LAKE | DRIVE

LAKE | DRIVE

JOE BAUMANN

Queer Space
A REBEL SATORI IMPRINT
New Orleans & New York

Published in the United States of America by
Queer Space
A Rebel Satori Imprint
www.rebelsatoripress.com

Book design: Sven Davisson

Paperback ISBN: 978-1-60864-272-4
Ebook ISBN: 978-1-60864-273-1

Library of Congress Control Number: 2023938552

For the book club: Emily, Tracey, Adeline, Danielle, and Julie.
Oh, fine. Jeff, too.

PART ONE

YOU

YOU'VE *seen how the world is. And you don't like it.*

It hasn't given you much. Famine, pain, disaster. Heartbreak. Death. You've seen it, felt it, lived it. It aches in your bones. It all mounts. Every day. The weight is plumb and heavy. It is a knot, sitting in your chest. Tumorous.

So you decide to change it. A transformation.

The change descends in silence, speedy and efficient. It is invisible and everywhere. Its claws—if they are claws; to you, they could be tentacles or stroking, loving hands, with tapered fingernails—dig into every building, cross every golf course, plunge into every pool. It goes everywhere, to deeper depths than even you can imagine. It finds things you cannot see. It slithers up nostrils and down throats, ekes through ears.

It snatches away. It leaves you breathless with possibility.

What does it take?

It takes mothers. And fathers. Brothers, uncles, criminals, saints, teachers, doctors. It takes line cooks and police officers. It takes people you will never meet. It takes DEA agents readying for stings. It takes airline pilots, pulling them from cockpits. It takes firefighters as they careen to a five-alarm blaze. It yanks away Olympians, erases MLB all-stars.

No one notices except you.

And, of course, the others.

R I O N

WHAT makes Rion a good server from the start is acting. Knowing how. It's all about finding the right depth of voice for each table, knowing how much to smile, when to joke. Knowing how to keep a grin on your face when some asshole keeps running you ragged or is clearly going to be a bad tipper or complains about something that is not your fault. Appearances are everything.

Lake | Drive is the only nice restaurant in Thomasville, too nice to actually be *in* Thomasville, located ten minutes outside of town among the St. Augustine grass and pin oaks that line highway six. During his interview for the job, Rion sits up straight, domes his hands on the table. Across from him Glenn, the owner, fires questions his way. Rion nails one about what appetizer he would recommend to a table: the onion rings. When Glenn raises an eyebrow, Rion leans back and says, "I know they're the least expensive appetizer. But onions are cheap. The overhead is low. I'm guessing they have the highest profit margin of anything on the menu."

He leaves with the job.

As a kid, Rion had dreamt of being an actor. Mostly for the money, he supposes now, and the fame, because he didn't really have any idea what it meant to take on a role. But his parents indulged his whim and signed him up for some amateur acting classes for children and let him attend drama camps during the summer even though his dad would have rather seen him playing soccer or baseball. He learned gesture, cues, affectation. He learned how to empty his head of himself and fill it with someone else. And that's what he does when he starts his training at Lake | Drive.

It only takes him a few days to realize that all of the front of house boys are sleeping with one another.

Donny says something first, a joke about Carter's uncut dick that turns out not to be a joke when Evan, the night bartender, confirms as much, waggling his eyebrows while mixing a champagne cocktail for one of Timothie's tables. Andre and Andrew slap each other's asses too much for it to be nothing, especially when Rion catches the former's fingers sliding too far between the creases of the latter's pants, which are admittedly snug and leave little of the derriere to the imagination. Rion's convictions are solidified when Doug, the salad guy, the only guy who works in the kitchen, catches Rion watching their games of grab-ass and says, handing him a pair of Waldorf salads to run to table eleven, "You know they're all fucking each other, right?"

Rion isn't sure what to say. Doug blinks at him. He's short and blond, but with a nice build; muscles pulse beneath his white t-shirt and matching apron that drapes all the way past his knees, veins beating against his smooth skin. Rion takes the salads to the table and offers to refill their water glasses, for which Timothie says thanks later because he was in the weeds because a nine-top couldn't figure out how to order fresh drinks all at once. Rion wonders, based on what Doug said and what he's seen, whether Timothie's wink is just a tired half-blink or if Timothie, who is tall and Grecian, with thick dark hair and nice dimples and shoulders that fill out his white Oxford nicely, would, in fact, like to sleep with him.

Lake | Drive is all windows and natural light. The front doors de-

3

posit diners into a baroque entryway with a coat check near the bathrooms, which are all brass fixtures and soft light, the porcelain scrubbed every hour by the bus boys, Micah and Toby, who grumble and hide the spray bottles filled with alien-blue sanitizer behind their backs as they march through the dining room toward their messy charges. Past the coat check is the host stand, a massive oak creation that looks like it belongs in the Oval Office rather than at the front of a restaurant with thirty tables, six of which pass in front of the small bar with its dozen stools and Megatouch gaming machine whose volume is kept locked on low so as not to interfere with the soft symphonies that pump through the restaurant's speakers. Past the bar is a large bump-out of a room that looks out on the water of Thomasville Lake, which is frightening in its clarity, a blue so shockingly crystalline you can practically see to the bottom. The quartet of tables in this area, Timothie has explained to Rion during training, are available by reservation only and features a prix fixe menu. Past the bump-out is the regular dining room, with booths lodged against the wall of windows as well as the opposite, plus two rows of tables in between. A private dining room used only for parties of at least twenty sits at the back of the restaurant. Everything is bleached blonde hardwood flooring and creamy white walls that match the tablecloths. The booths are wiped down after each seating, their chocolate leather practically gleaming like a new car.

Because he spent two years in high school as a busser/host when he abandoned his dreams of the big screen and the Broadway stage, Rion is subjected to only three days of server training at Lake | Drive rather than the usual week and a half. Glenn says this to him as if it's the greatest gift in the world. He is a big man, Glenn, always dressed in a rumpled Oxford that chokes at his throat until he unbuttons the collar after the dinner rush ends, when he settles in at the bar for a Dewars neat, which Evan pours without prompting. His cheeks are ruddy, juggly; Glenn has certainly bought into the notion that guests will never trust a skinny cook. The first two days of Rion's training are mostly memorizing the menu, which is small, the focus on meat and potatoes as well as a hearty supply of high-end, exotic-sounding vegetables. This is because, as Glenn has explained, even though Thomasville is squarely in northern Missouri and full of plenty of down-home folks who are most interested in mashed potatoes and sirloins, the fancy liberal arts college in town—where most of his staff are students—is home to enough pot-smoking hippies and yuppy vegan humanities professors that they go apeshit for his haricot verts and mustard greens and mache and sorrel. Rion learns fast, especially when he doesn't have to instill in his head all of the low-brow side dishes (Lake | Drive offers only potatoes au gratin, small Caesars, baked potatoes and their sweet cousins, frites, and a homemade slaw) and three dozen kinds of salad dressing ("We serve balsamic, Italian, and, begrudgingly, ranch," Glenn said). Then there is the Point of Sales system, which he breezes through, and the table numbers, easy enough. By day three, which is all food running and expo, Rion is practically waiting on tables on his own. His final test is doing so while Glenn sits at the bar, drink in one hand, pen in the other, watching Rion's every move. Timothie, who trains him, looms nearby, eyes unblinking.

One of the first things he noticed about Lake | Drive wasn't its weird name, which was a reference to both the pristine lake onto which its vista of windows gazes and the restaurant's quirky schtick of having, like the bump-out room, an expensive prix fixe—pricier than the bump-out room's—available on the weekends at a table situated at a gazebo located a tenth of a mile from the restaurant proper, to which both eaters and server arrive via golf cart. No, what attracted Rion's attention are the weird gender lines along which the restaurant operates: the bartender and host and servers are all men, except for Angela, a tall, willowy woman who closes the dining room; the back-of-house, the dishwasher and line cooks and expo lead, are all women who wear their white coats buttoned up tight, hair pulled back behind thick bandanas. The exception there is Doug, the all-seeing eye of the salad station.

"What's the deal with that?" Rion asks Timothie as he finishes up his last shift of training, having passed Glenn's exam with flying colors. Not a perfect score—eventually, Timothie tells Rion that no one has ever earned a perfect score on that initial evaluation—but pretty close, Rion's only blemishes a failure to inquire with specificity about the table's potential interest in dessert as well as a shaky refilling of their glasses of petite sirah, two droplets staining the white tablecloth.

"It's just what Glenn does," Timothie says, leaning against the counter at the front server's station, wedging himself between the coffee urn and a pitcher of sweetened iced tea that was sweating onto its napkin and saucer. "He thinks women are better cooks and men are better talkers."

"Seems antiquated."

Timothie shrugs. "No one's complained yet."

"And what if a woman wants to be a server?"

"He finds a reason not to hire them. Or convinces them that grilling steaks is more impressive. He pays them well."

The first three weeks fly by. Rion falls into the rhythms of summer: waking up late in his empty apartment, his roommate gone for eight weeks to an internship at the Capitol in Jefferson City; hitting the McClain State recreation center in the morning, sweating off the cocktails he drinks at the Lake | Drive bar every night after his shifts are over; lazing around until three-thirty, when he changes and walks out the door to drive to the restaurant; works his shifts, every day acclimating himself more and more to the movements and nuances of the restaurant.

The money at Lake | Drive is good; appetizers are pricey, and the wines are pricier. The few college students who come in order Bud Lights and fried oysters and tip well because they all know at least someone who works there and don't want to get bad reputations. Because it's summer, the clientele is mostly bored history and business faculty as well as the cadre of surprisingly well-to-do real estate moguls who somehow make good enough money only an hour south of Ottumwa, Iowa, to afford expensive bone-in tomahawk steaks and scallopini. Though there's no official dress code, men wear suit coats and women pearl earrings. One man accosts him gently for not knowing Haydn from Beethoven—soft symphonic strings pump out through speakers, often drowned out by the drone of voices—but still tips over twenty percent, laughing with his tablemates at Rion's ignorance. For the sake of paying his bills, Rion laughs along, too, but doesn't offer to-go boxes for anyone who hasn't finished their porterhouses. They congeal fat and blood on their plates in dark, oozing rings.

He enjoys the work. Things are great. His desk is strewn with stacks of cash.

And then, after twenty-one days at Lake | Drive, it happens: the disappearances.

TIMOTHIE

TIMOTHIE isn't in love with the new guy. Yes, he has nice dimples, and the kind of pale American skin that burns easily in the sun before darkening to a slight tan. Rion also has good forearms, with thick, twitchy muscles and green worms for veins. He carries pint glasses three at a time, eschewing the drink trays except for when it comes to glasses of wine and cocktails, which fat-ass Glenn has declared a requirement for serving for reasons Timothie doesn't understand but doesn't feel like getting into an argument about. Beer and sodas he'll let you carry by hand so long as you don't tend to slosh, but anything fancier has to, for who-the-hell-knows reasons, be delivered on a black tray held at chest height, each drink settled down on the diner's right side at two o'clock. Rion, with his long fingers like a piano player's, doesn't dribble or slosh a drop. Timothie realizes quickly that he has little to teach him, so he glides Rion through his training days with little instruction, feeling bored.

The day of the disappearances, a Wednesday, Timothie is scheduled for a double-shift, lunch plus early-out on the dinner schedule, the four pm starter. His favorite pair of shifts because the four pm gets the section with two booths and a pair of four-tops that easily get shoved together for bigger parties. Plus, the side work is front station, easy-peasy as long as you remember to refill the tea pitchers and don't run out of coffee. End of the night, just fill up a tub with hot water for soaking condiment lids and you're out of there as fast as you can fill your sugar caddies.

God, the place is ridiculous. Glenn can't decide if he wants to cater to potato farmers or provosts. He somehow manages to do both, though, and he doesn't give Timothie a hard time because for as laid back and easy to boss around as Donny and Carter and the others are, none of them are as good at schmoozing as Timothie is, and Glenn knows it. And Timothie knows Glenn knows it. So Glenn doesn't ever yell at Timothie and he makes sure the kitchen staff don't give Timothie any guff. It's why Glenn hands over the newbies to Timothie for training, because when they've been put under Timothie's wing like Andrew and Andre have, they turn out far better. The fact that Timothie tends to sleep with them within the first two weeks of their employ, well, Glenn doesn't worry about it so long as no one complains, and so far no one has. Timothie likes to think this is because he's as good in bed as he is on the dining room floor. Better, maybe, which sure is saying something.

Rion is tough, though. Timothie has figured out over the last few years that college guys tend to be far more flexible with their sexual preferences than they like to pretend. At the very least, they tend to be curious. A couple of beers, a disclaimer that nothing you might do with them has to mean anything, especially if they don't like it, and it's easy enough to get their pants off. But for all of Timothie's overt flirtations with Rion over the first few weeks, including picking up the tab for his after-shift drinks more than once and making overt interludes to the idea that they could hang out after they're finished at the Lake | Drive bar, have gone without response. And Timothie isn't being subtle. And Rion doesn't seem stupid. He seems, worse, uninterested.

On the day of the disappearances the apartment is empty when

9

Timothie wakes up, which is weird, not just because his roommate, Flower, who works at Temera's Ephemeras on the downtown square, is never up before eleven, but because the apartment is empty-empty. As in, her stuff is gone: the futon that she contributed even though it clashes with the rich darkness of his leather couch and the mahogany coffee table. The artwork she hung on the walls—all garbage she sketched when she was in high school, weird amorphous blobs that she's convince are impressionism but really just look like something any third grader with a colored pencil could do—has been removed. Her bedroom is a cavern, totally empty minus dust bunnies. Not even any indentations in the carpet where her bed dug into the floor or her desk sat. All the stemware—she loved vintage wine glasses—strewn in the kitchen cabinets, all of the plates and bowls she'd supplied, scrounged from the Good Will on the downtown square. Even the food she bought last weekend, the milk and eggs and individually-wrapped processed cheeses and the artisanal stuffed mushrooms. All of it gone.

He tries calling her, but the phone line's been disconnected, a monotone woman's recorded voice exhorting him to hang up.

Perplexed, Timothie showers—her shampoos, her Venus brand razor, the bath salts she keeps behind the toilet tank all gone—and dresses. He glances into her bedroom one last time, concerned but unsure what to do. When they met as freshmen, Flower said her parents were dead and that she'd been raised by a bitch of an aunt whom she was thrilled to have escaped thanks to her full-ride scholarship; even though Flower was hippie-dippie, running around campus barefoot in sheer sundresses, never seeming to actually go to class, she was crazy smart, it turned out, taking advanced biology and chemistry classes as a freshman because she'd rocked AP and had actually dual enrolled at a decent community college when she was a junior in high school. She was on track to graduate in, like, two and a half years with a degree in organic chemistry or something. Timothie could never keep it straight. He was majoring in communications because it was easy and he looked good on camera.

The commute to Lake | Drive bores Timothie. He's seen the scutch grass and silver maples hundreds of times by now, passed the empty rolling fields interrupted by the periodic derelict farmhouse that are probably now meth labs on endless occasions. But then the lake appears, a bloom of almost-clear water surrounded by vibrant greenery and, eventually, the parking lot to the restaurant. Timothie has a penchant for marching in through the kitchen door right before his shift is set to begin, an hour before the front doors unlock for lunch. Glenn always shakes his head but smiles as he scribbles instructions for Merebeth about that day's house special. Lake | Drive doesn't have such a thing as a lead server, but it might as well be Timothie; he knows how to combine the right bit of sass with deference, how to be demure and demanding in the proper proportion depending on the attitude of the guests he's waiting on. And he knows his wine pairings, as well as ideal recommendations for salad-appetizer-entrée-dessert orderings, when guests are starved and want to chow down. Glenn, of course, would never say any of this. He's not the type to give out compliments so much as just glare less frequently than normal.

Today, though, Glenn's nowhere to be found.

The prep cooks—three for the morning, along with Merebeth—are busy stocking their stations and mixing fresh batches of the house balsamic. Two other servers are scheduled for lunch: Andre and Andrew. Scott will man the bar until Evan clocks in at five.

"Where's Glenn?" Timothie says to Andrew when he comes into the kitchen carrying an empty cutting board streaked with lemon seeds and slithers of juice.

Andrew, short and stocky with a bumpy complexion but nice smile—and great abs, as Timothie learned during the last staff Christmas party when half the staff, drunk on Patron and Stoli, peeled off their ugly holiday sweaters and tossed themselves into the Days Inn's indoor pool—frowns and glances toward the small office near the back door. "Something's wrong." Andrew's voice is deep, like the shock of a cold pond. "Something about his wife being missing."

"Oh," Timothie says. He thinks of Flower, considers saying something but then doesn't.

"Something else is going on," Andrew says.

"What do you mean?"

"Something weird happened with Andre's philosophy class."

Like many of the students working at Lake | Drive, Andre is in summer school, not because he failed anything during the academic year but because he wants to get some credits out of the way and justify sticking around Thomasville when most sane twenty-somethings would be heading back to St. Louis or Kansas City or even Des Moines for two and a half months of alcohol and casual sex.

The problem, Andre explains as he spreads tablecloths and uses his crumber to iron out any bumps, is that today someone new was teaching his class. Andre keeps his hair cropped short using clippers he keeps in his apartment bathroom—Timothie spent the night there, right before finals—which is tidy, all white tile and white vanity and white paint dotted with his shaved-off hairs. He played football in high school and still has the quads and cheekbones of a wide receiver, Caribbean skin he inherited from his mother. He licks his lips when he speaks, as if he has to wipe away the periods and pauses.

"What do you mean?" Timothie says.

"It wasn't our usual professor."

"And he didn't explain?"

"She," Andre says, blinking at Timothie, who is polishing a steak knife. "And no. No one asked anything about it or seemed confused, either."

"What?"

"They just went along, talking to this woman—Dr. Axelrod was her name—as if she'd been teaching the class all summer. She knew everyone's names, too."

"That's weird."

"And at the end of class I went to the division office and asked what was going on and the woman working the desk looked at me like I was the crazy person." He arranged peach cloth napkins containing silverware in decorative heaps on his tables. "She had no idea what I was talking about. Didn't even recognize my real professor's name."

Timothie nods, pulling water glasses from the rack he has dragged from the dish station. The glass is warm to the touch, hot from the Hobart. One of them is smudged, and he rubs at the mark with the edge of the tablecloth, leaving the glass sparkling. He sets it down, nudging it into alignment with the others.

"The really weird thing," Andre is saying, " is that when I went and looked on the college website, there was no evidence my professor even existed."

Timothie thinks of Flower, how every minute piece of her had been excised from the apartment, even her pain in the ass hairs that would clog the bathtub drain. The plunger with its pink rubber end that she made jokes about being a sex toy. Even the yellow flower she'd drawn onto the television remote with nail polish: he hadn't seen it when he was grabbing his keys from their spot on the end table. Timothie pictures himself scrubbed out of the apartment. What would he leave behind? Or: what marks would disappear? His tv? The poster of Starry Night he hung over his bed before realizing how cliché that was? He feels a plumb weight in his stomach as he spreads his last tablecloth.

"And now this thing with Rhoda," Andre says, gesturing toward the kitchen. Rhoda, Glenn's wife, who usually shows up right before the lunch rush, a bandana tied around her head. Rhoda, always throwing herself on the line to help Merebeth or whichever cook is backed up. Rhoda with her long red hair and her penchant for well vodka and Sprite, which she'll drink while massaging Glenn's massive back after the dinner rush is finally over even though everyone knows he's spent the night schmoozing with guests while she toiled over steaks, burning her fingers on plates she pulls from the salamander with her bare hands. Rhoda, who has been at Lake | Drive every single day that Timothie has worked a shift, even the time it turned out she had the flu and spread it around to all of the kitchen staff and half of the front of house; Timothie, with his robust immune system, only caught the sniffles and one night of fever, which didn't strike him down until after his evening's side work was finished, his silverware rolled, and which broke before his next shift had arrived. He probably still managed to infect a few guests, but he hoped, at the time, that it was only the bad tippers and impatient soda drinkers who demanded fresh diet cokes every three minutes.

"What happened to her?" Timothie asks. But he's pretty sure he knows the answer.

Andre, his gaze turned out toward the water, voice drifting away like the waves chopping toward the lake's middle, says, "She's gone."

A N D R E W

ANDREW thought, when he toured the apartment complex and then signed the lease immediately, that he would love the pool. The complex is the only one in Thomasville with that feature, a rectangle of hyper-chlorinated water that sits inside the ring of the horseshoe-shaped building that looks more like a Super 8 than anywhere anyone would want to live. But the units are nice, hardwood floors and upgraded appliances, even marble countertops and an open floor plan. The one-bedroom he chose is inexpensive enough that, after paying his rent with his Lake | Drive tips, he has plenty of leftover cash for booze and eating out and even splurging on a cheap cable package.

But the pool tricked Andrew. Instead of being a feature that appeals to his dreams of late-night dips and inviting the server crew over to drink cheap beers at one of the glass-topped tables and then cannonball into the deep end, all the pool does is make him think of his sister.

The first time she suffered an episode they were on family vacation, somewhere in the northeast, a tiny salt-sprayed town that was all bed and breakfasts and rocky outcroppings, two-lane cobblestone streets and locally-owned diners. Andrew was twelve, Jessica seventeen. Even though they were on the Atlantic, the ocean roiling only a hundred yards from the Cape Cod they'd rented for the week, the house had a pool that Andrew had spent every waking hour of the first three days in. On the fourth, though, he woke to his sister screaming that there were men in the water. Her voice was a ragged shock, the screech of it so hard and throaty he expected her to start coughing up blood.

Outside, the pool, a simple rectangular in-ground, was serene and empty, the only movement the slightest surface ripple from a breeze, the only thing in the water a plastic ring Andrew had not fished out yesterday before he was done swimming. Andrew›s parents, both standing at the edge of the water, looked from where Jessica was pointing to each other and then to her. When they asked what she meant by men in the water, she only grew more hysterical.

They cut the trip short because no matter what anyone said Jessica refused to believe that there weren›t two men sitting in the deep-end, cross-legged on the floor of the pool. She went practically rabid when Andrew tried to get in the water, her shrieks so animal and terrible their parents were sure a neighbor would call the police. Jessica whimpered the entire drive back to Missouri, which they completed without stopping except for restroom and food breaks. Andrew sulked the whole time, casting daggered glances across the back seat at his sister, his parents taking turns driving so the other could rest, though neither of them managed any sleep.

Back home, Jessica seemed better, as though she had been haunted acutely by the pool at the vacation home. She settled down, caught her breath. Their parents gently suggested she see a therapist, but Jessica shook this idea off and they, not sure how to handle whatever was happening to their seventeen-year-old, acquiesced. Everything seemed fine until the end of summer when Jessica went to the public pool with some friends and arrived home only a few hours later, sobbing and wailing about seeing people beneath the inflated lily pads that kids tried to traverse, arms gripping drooping cargo nets strung above their heads. Both of their parents were at work, so Andrew was left to his own devices to try to calm Jessica down, who'd been dumped at the front door by her friends. She was incomprehensible, trying to speak through gluey tears and hiccups. He pieced together that she was sure the men in the pool were the same ones that had been at their vacation home, and she was freaked out by the idea that she was being followed.

Thus began a flurry of psychotherapists and failed treatments. Doctors and psychiatrists were flummoxed. At first, they thought it was schizophrenia, but Jessica was adamant that she didn't hear any voices; the men never spoke to her. They didn't even acknowledge her presence or that she could see them. One doctor postulated Charles Bonnet syndrome, but when optometrists and neurologists tested her vision and optic nerve, there was no damage. His sister insisted that the men only appeared in water, which made every specialist she saw shrug. Eventually, a general diagnosis of ongoing psychosis was settled upon.

On the day of the disappearances, Andrew makes it through his shift unscathed; he waits on his tables, only mildly distracted by Timothie's story about Flower and the fact that Rhoda has vanished. He avoids Glenn, who lumbers through the dining room like a bulldozer, once actually knocking into Scott and sending the last dregs of a half-finished rum and coke spilling down his shirt. Poor Scott blinks at the mess and attempts to wipe it away, but a brown mark remains stained against his torso throughout the rest of the lunch rush, which seems normal enough. Throughout the day, other Lake | Drive employees share discoveries of the disappeared: the regulars who come in for midweek steaks and martinis never show for their standing one pm reservation; Perry's neighbors, who are always outside on their porch swing, have been replaced by some young couple with a toddler that he didn't recognize when he took out the trash; one of the busboys noticed that the mailman who delivers his mail was gone.

During the mid-afternoon lull, when the floor is cut down to just Timothie, the servers are standing around in the kitchen, waiting for Cynthia to run the last batch of silverware through the Hobart. Doug, at the edge of their messy circle, says, "Have you all noticed that no one else seems to think anything's wrong?"

Everyone stares at him. Andrew wonders if anyone from his life has disappeared, and he feels a cold shock of worry for his sister. When he's climbing the stairs to his unit hours later that night he sees a stranger unlock the door to the apartment next door where he should see Phil, a man in his thirties who has lived there longer than Andrew. He decides this must mean Jessica is fine; surely no one has two people close to them—either by physical or emotional proximity—disappear. That would just be cruel.

"You're right," Rion says.

Evan folds his arms over his chest. "But that doesn't make any sense." He wears chunky glasses and resembles Buddy Holly, though he's more twitchy and a terrible singer, as evidenced by the one night the staff convinced Glenn to try karaoke; Evan got wasted on whiskey sours and tried to sing "Don't Stop Believin'" and didn't hit a single note on-key. The next day he pretended not to remember.

"Does any of this make sense?" Rion says.

"I guess not. But why would we remember? What makes us special?"

"Well, we all work here," Doug says.

"We're waiters," Andre says, "not, like, superheroes."

"Definitely not saints," Donny says, elbowing Carter.

Andrew extricates himself from the conversation to drop off a check at his last table, a pair of dowagers in their best finery. He has no idea where they've come from. Thomasville isn't home to anything of particular note aside from the university, and these two women don't have the air of emeritus faculty or vice provosts or whatever; they give off Maggie Smith in *Downton Abbey* vibes, particularly in that they haven't spoken a single complete sentence to him during their entire meal, hushing their tittered conversation as soon as he comes near, as if he might overhear their deepest, darkest secrets. But when they clear out, their champagne flutes empty and their bowls of cobb salad impressively wiped clean, each has tipped him well, one of them even writing *Thank you* in flourished handwriting beneath her signature on the credit card slip. He wonders if anyone has disappeared from their lives today.

The summer evening is a blaze of reddish pink when Andrew clocks out, leaving Timothie and Angela behind as the only two servers still on the clock. The others are huddled at the bar, drinking away their tip money. They're all bleary and slouched, tired despite the fact that their bodies are used to pounding through the kitchen and dining room.

"It's all fucked up," Donny is saying, voice already slurred. He's drinking long island iced teas with shitty well alcohol and is on his third.

"Maybe we're all just dreaming," Carter says. "Maybe I'm dreaming and none of you are real."

"Who's the philosopher now?" Andre says.

"Which one was it that said the whole brains in a vat thing?" Donny says.

"Descartes," Andre says, shaking his head. "But it's a modern bastardization. Really, Descartes' whole thing was about a demon or something."

"Or something? Aren't you taking a class?"

"Yeah, it's intro-level. We haven't gone that deep."

Evan sets down a round of shots, something that reeks of tequila and tastes like warmed puke. Andrew coughs and tries not to regurgitate it. His hands feel slimy.

"Has anyone checked the news?" he says.

Eyes swivel toward him. "The news?" Andre says.

Donny pulls out his phone and starts typing. Everyone stares at him. Evan pours a Bells from the tap, setting it down on the serving mat just before Angela whisks it away to her six-top at the back of the dining room. They split an expensive bottle of Beaujolais as an appetizer and two of them have been one-upping each other buying drinks; they've reached top-shelf margaritas, which cost fourteen dollars each. Perry, the host, finishes wiping down his floor chart and calls out a goodbye as he leaves through the front. One of the busboys comes around behind the bar and takes the bus tub that Evan has filled with plates and pint glasses.

"Nothing," Donny says. The blue glow of the screen lights up his chin, which is covered in day-old stubble despite the Lake | Drive policy against facial hair. No one has been paying attention, what with Rhoda gone. "I'm not finding anything."

Andrew eventually slips away after forking over cash for his drinks; he's only had two beers and the nasty, flammable shot, so his feet are solid under him. Nonetheless, Andre follows him out of the restaurant and claps a hand on his shoulder, saying, "You okay to drive?"

"Yes." Andrew doesn't turn to look at him. The night is sticky, the bugs thick against lampposts and darting toward his ears and nostrils. He knows he should call his parents, check on his sister. He knows he should want to do these things. But another part of him just wants to look out at the pool, its underwater lights turning everything neon blue, the water rippling with night breeze. He wants to look and make sure that he doesn't see anyone lurking beneath the surface.

But another part of him wants to be with Andre, and this part over-whelms. So when Andre's hand moves to Andrew's trapezius muscle and starts kneading, Andrew doesn't tell him to stop.

"Tired?" Andre says.

Andrew turns to him. "Yes. But no."

Andre smiles. "Good."

D O ꊿ ꊿ Y

OF all people, it's fucking Doug, the loser salad bitch who still hasn't passed muster with Glenn for a chance to work front of house, who figures it out. Donny, who is pretty damn smart—he scored a fourteen hundred on the SAT, hello—has been outdone by god damn Doug.

Somehow, he's the one to piece together that it is only the employees at Lake | Drive who know that anything is amiss. When he turned on the television the morning after the disappearances, Doug explains, the wrong man was president. A different face splashed across Fox and CNN and ABC. When he hopped onto the internet to find out why, there was no evidence that the former guy existed; his name had been scrubbed away completely. No Twitter account, no angry Facebook pages in support and in hatred. No weird InfoWars or Occupy Democrats hit pieces. No Republicans and Democrats at one another's throats over him. Instead, they were at each other's throats over another straight old white guy who looked ready to croak in the next several months.

Donny doesn't mind hearing this, really, because the former guy was a fucking idiot, over-tanned, unable to form a coherent sentence; he looked like he wore his pants backward and was maybe in a diaper half the time. Not that this new guy—he recognizes him, at least, when Doug says the name; it's not some rando geriatric fuck—is much better. He mumbles, drinks water with two hands on the glass, stutters and forgets peoples' names, mixing up his mom and his sister, if the clips Donny finds on YouTube are anything to judge by.

Doug's eyes are buggy as he explains, as if his life will somehow be changed dramatically under this new president. Donny doesn't really care about politics, local or global; he just wants to be left the fuck alone. So, the fact that the president has disappeared doesn't really faze him much. He'll learn over the course of several days that other world leaders have been blinked out of existence, replaced by other people with European and Latin and Chinese names he can't pronounce. One person for another. What concerns him after Doug explains his theory is whether his weed dealer still exists, and he's relieved when he sends a text—*Any good baseball games on tonight?*—and immediately gets a response: *Cubs are on at 7.* Thank fucking god, because finding someone with drugs in northern Missouri that aren't made from Sudafed or Drano is nearly impossible. He wants to get high every now and then, not rot his teeth and develop an addiction to scrubbing his bathtub. Plus, Annette is hot, all ice-blonde hair and perfect tits that she shows off in tank tops, even in winter.

The only table in the restaurant is a pair of large men in overalls who are gnawing on bloody ribeyes that they quite seriously asked be cooked for one minute on each side. When Donny brought them out, swimming in blood, the men nodded, one asking for Heinz 57 and the other a bottle of A-1. Donny nodded and watched as the men dumped half of the contents onto their meat, then doused their loaded baked potatoes, too.

"I asked everyone I saw," Doug says, pulling a chilled bowl from the small refrigerator beneath his station. "'Who is the president of the US?'" He shakes his head. "I sounded like a crazy person."

"Uh huh," Donny says.

"But literally no one said the right answer." He keeps shaking his head. Donny wants to reach out and slap him or cup his jaw and hold it steady. "I started to wonder if I was wrong, you know?"

Doug asks Donny who the president is. To fuck with him, Donny says the new guy. When Doug's eyes go big, Donny laughs and says, "Just kidding."

Doug wilts. All evening, he asks the same question by way of greeting.

He's convinced, by the end of the dinner rush, that it's the fucking rapture. Or something like that.

"Well, maybe not the biblical version."

"The biblical version?" Donny says, swiping a credit card at the PoS computer nestled between Doug's station and the ice machine. Fucking couple decides they want only their rum runners and some bread and that's it. Meanwhile, Timothie is working the bump-out, making oodles of cash simply because Glenn has christened him his chosen one. Doug is building a cobb. Donny watches him shake out a fistful of shredded romaine and iceberg, then covers it in bleu cheese crumbles and tomatoes while yelling out that he's ready for the cubed chicken.

"Cubed chicken coming," Wendy calls out from the line. Her voice is warm and loud, managing to ring out over the sound of sizzling steaks and roiling fryers.

Doug turns toward Wendy but keeps talking to Donny. "Yeah, the biblical version. A bunch of people rise up into the air, ascending into heaven before the devil takes over and turns earth into hell? You know?"

"I think he's already done that," Donny says.

"It's the second coming of Jesus and the salvation of both the living and the dead."

"So we should be seeing zombies or something?"

"Unclear. But people should be literally ascending to heaven."

"So we should see people, like, flying and shit?"

"Kind of," Doug says. "I haven't been to bible study in a while."

"You used to do bible study?"

Doug dips a ladle into the balsamic dressing and fills a ramekin, then shoves the salad toward Donny. "This is for table twenty-two."

"Thanks."

"The word isn't actually anywhere in the New Testament."

"What word?"

"Rapture."

"Read it a lot lately?" Donny turns to leave the kitchen.

"No," Doug says, as an order for three house salads spews out from the wheel. "I googled it this morning. You should try it."

Donny delivers the salad and the check, takes an order from a three-top—two steaks with frites and a Reuben sandwich—and then checks in with his five-top, who are ready for a second round of drinks and all want the tempeh and garden veggie salad, two with balsamic and three with ranch dressing. He punches in the order—three pints of Pale Ale, a pair of pinot grigios for the drinks—and while he waits for Evan to pour, he slips back into the kitchen. Merebeth is screaming something about a porterhouse that's sending up smoke and a chicken breast that looks like it's been through a house fire. Wendy is shaking her head.

"So, there's no dead rising. How is it the rapture?" he says to Doug.

Doug wipes down his station, gathering a few shreds of parmesan and a stray diced tomato in his hand. "What else could it be?"

"No one went floating into the fucking sky, far as I can tell."

"Unless they did in the middle of the night."

"Wouldn't we see reports of, like, empty gravesites or something?"

"Would that be newsworthy?"

25

"Baby pandas being born in China are, like, front-page news. I'm pretty sure the dead disappearing would make headlines."

"A new president didn't."

Timothie goes swishing by with a tray full of entrees balanced atop one palm. He hip-checks the swinging door and yells, "Coming through," even though the door is one-way; everyone knows you enter on the right so you don't crash the fuck into anyone. Donny rolls his eyes. It's not that Timothie is a bad guy—he's certainly not a bad lay, that's for sure, happy to bottom if need be, and with Donny, that is a need be—he's just annoying in his showiness. Like, dude, we all know you're good at what you do. Chill out.

"So, then, what's up?" Donny says, folding his arms and watching while Doug portions out salad mix. "What's your theory?"

"I think we're the only ones who know."

"We?"

"The restaurant," Doug says. He turns and gestures toward the women cooking, Cynthia in the dish pit, Glenn, who has just stepped out of the office, red-eyed and silent. "Lake | Drive. I think only people who work here have any idea anything happened at all."

"How would that work?"

Doug shrugs. "I don't know. Maybe someone chose us."

CARTER

EVERYONE *has secrets*, Carter thinks every night as he gets out of his car and marches around the side of the house, feet swishing through the dewy grass that his father has, once again, let grow too long. He walks through the backyard, down the slight slope of a hill to the furthest reaches of the property where the yurt waits. He pulls the canvas away, steps inside, and turns on the battery-powered SUBOOS tent lamp, which casts harsh LED light across the small table and the beds. His twin brother, Micha, groans on the top bunk and rolls away from the shine.

Carter's not a liar, exactly. He is a student at McClain State, he is studying biology. What he hasn't told anyone at Lake | Drive or in Phi Kappa Gamma—or anyone else, for that matter—is that he's a *townie*. He hates the word; it sends spikes of anger up and down his spine every time one of his friends says it, because it's always a curse, a spat-out insult. It's not like it's Carter's fault that he was born in Thomasville and didn't get out, mostly because McClain would have him and have him on the cheap because his mother works in the alumni office. Mostly it's also because his twin brother didn't want to leave either, didn't want to go any further than the yurt that's been his sanctuary since he was nine. Carter's the only one who has ever been able to calm Micha, to keep him from letting out high whines when he's anxious or angry or sad or scared or confused, whines that leave adults ready to tear out their

27

hair, including his parents, who, when Carter and Micha were children, responded by slamming doors and shouting at one another, at Micha, at Carter, before pulling bottles of wine from the fridge and hardly bothering to pour them into glasses as they started drinking.

Carter sets his apron down on the tiny table and sits. He pulls his tip money from his pocket, letting the heap fan out on the table. Unlike his co-workers, he waits until he's arrived at home to count his evening's take. If Micha isn't sleeping, he'll want to count it, and he can always tell when Carter has already done so on his own. Carter always waits, no matter how many times Donny calls him a weirdo or Timothie clucks his tongue when Carter shrugs and won't share whether he's made twenty percent on his sales.

The only sounds in the yurt is the hum of the mini-fridge and the wet noise of his brother's breathing. The yurt is humid thanks to its lack of air conditioning, but a night breeze is filtering through the vent flaps cut high in the canvas, which alleviates some of the heat. Carter knows that no one would blame him if he started sleeping in the house again; he's twenty-one years old, for god's sake, and he shouldn't be beholden to his autistic brother's whims. But if he doesn't look out for Micha, who will? The last time his parents even asked about Micha was a week ago, when Carter crossed their path in the kitchen while he was raiding the refrigerator for milk. They didn't castigate him for taking the food; they seem to understand that this is part of the deal: Carter will take on the guardianship role if they will supply the sustenance. They seem happy to abide this.

Seventy-three dollars. Not a bad haul, especially considering the blonde bitch who complained that her malbec wasn't chilled (what?) and that her portobello salad had mushrooms in it (what?), and that her sticky toffee pudding was too warm (what?), and who paid instead of her red-cheeked husband, a bald balloon of a man who wouldn't look Carter in the eye even when he pointed out that his whiskey sour was one of the best he'd ever had and that his t-bone steak had been cooked to perfection. She'd left him a nine-dollar tip on a seventy dollar tab.

Micha stirs, turning to face the interior of the yurt. His hands are tucked up under the pillow that he's slept on since he was a kid, its interior worn down to the thickness of a pancake. He blinks and says, "Hi, brother."

"Hi, brother."

"Good night?"

"Good enough."

Carter watches Micha lick his lips and look at the money. "I'd have waited to count it, but I thought you were asleep."

Micha nods but says nothing. He yawns, then rolls back over without another word.

The first thing Carter wondered when the disappearances happened was whether his brother was still around. For just a moment, while listening to Doug explain, a tiny part of him hoped that Micha was gone.

He feels bad about it, but he can't help it. The impulse, while unfair, sat fat like an egg in his gut. He'd stayed over at Donny's apartment the night before, and they spent a languorous Wednesday in bed until they both had to go straight to Lake | Drive for their dinner shifts. Carter showered at Donny's, aware that Micha would probably freak out; he knew Carter's schedule, waited for him to arrive at the yurt when his shifts were over, ready to be drawn from his sleepy malaise. Carter had felt the tiniest bit of extra pleasure as the water cascaded over him, not simply because of what Donny's fingers were busy doing with his ass but because of the thought of his brother freaking out. He was just

29

tired of being trapped by his brother's needs. What about his own?

And so, as Doug outlined his theories about the disappearances, Carter's mind first went to his brother, the thought *I hope Micha has disappeared* slicing into his head before he could stop himself. And there it sat all night until he clocked out, when Donny made eyes at him. When Carter shook his head, said he was tired. Donny said, "Since when has that stopped you?" Carter mumbled, faked a yawn, and said he could use a night in his own bed. He drove home through the dark too fast, his heart pounding. When he opened the flap and stepped into the yurt and turned on the light and found his brother exactly where he would always be, he felt a mix of relief and disappointment.

Even though his feet are throbbing and his lower back feels like it's full of needles, Carter pulls a Natural Light from the mini-fridge that, like the lights, runs thanks to a small generator that his parents invested in several years ago after Micha got sick drinking curdled milk he'd secretly hoarded in the yurt. When they were kids, Micha had an inexplicable obsession with the arrangement of food, freaking out if his mother stocked the fridge or pantry not to his specifications, which he could never articulate and whose patterns Carter couldn't crack. After weeks of tantrums following her trips to the grocery store, their mother finally said, "Fine, you do it," to Micha and, leaving the bags on the kitchen table, marched into the living room and tossed herself down on the couch. Carter watched Micha, who froze for a long moment as he stared at the bags full of canned beans and Wonder Bread and boxed cereal. Then something unlatched in his brother and Micha went nuts, pulling everything out of the freezer, rearranging tubs of ice cream and frozen pizzas and blocks of ground beef wrapped in aluminum foil. An hour later, the refrigerator was topsy-turvy, milk shoved next to mustard and ranch dressing, the deli cutlets stuffed in the spot where eggs belonged, baby carrots in the cheese drawer. The pantry underwent a similar chaotic reorganization, Cheerios and uncooked pasta hanging out next to each other, canned peas and green beans buddied up with packets of taco seasoning.

"Whatever," their mother said when she surveyed the wares. "As long as he's not howling."

The one beer, which he drinks fast, makes Carter woozy for sleep, but when he lies down on the lower bunk, he can't fall asleep. On the occasions Micha is deeply asleep and doesn't wake up upon Carter's arrival, Carter sneaks up to the house, slipping through the kitchen's sliding door and prowling upstairs to his bedroom and the full-size bed there with an actual mattress and quilty blankets and air conditioning. But he has to be careful about it. Micha has caught him leaving before, sitting up fast and bellowing out questions about where Carter is heading. He has to make up something on the spot—usually he pretends he needs to take a piss and will be back soon—and is forced back into the yurt, because if Micha discovers that he's alone he'll lose it, screeching and punching the canvas or pummeling his mattress, sending the frame of the bunk beds wobbling with such careening that Carter will spend the next morning checking all of the bolts and screws to make sure the thing isn't about to collapse.

Carter blinks through the dark at his brother and decides not to risk it. He lowers himself into the bottom bunk and covers himself with only the top sheet. He sweats and thinks of all the people who have vanished—who knows how many—and regrets, with a sourness that keeps him awake all night—his desire for his brother to blink out of existence.

On Friday morning, they make their weekly trip to Temera's Ephemeras. The consignment store sits on the northeast corner of the downtown square, taking up the equivalent of two storefronts, neighbors with one of the dive bars that doesn't card and thus to which freshmen and sophomores flock on the weekends. The square is home to two Chinese restaurants, two coffee shops, a three-screen theatre, one bookstore. The DMV shut down two years ago, and now everyone who needs a fresh license has to drive to Columbia, an hour and a half trek down state highway 63, which is usually crammed with farm equipment and semis heading back from depositing supplies in Ottumwa.

Carter is worried that Micha will notice that Flower, the girl who always works Friday mornings and slips his brother Andes candies from the glass bowl at the register with a cardstock sign reading "10c EACH," is gone; he's prepared for a meltdown, given that he knows that Flower was one of the ones who disappeared, attested to by Timothie. But when Micha enters the store in front of Carter, he waves at the woman standing behind the jewelry counter-slash-checkout-lane. She's younger-looking than Flower, probably sixteen or seventeen, with strawberry blonde hair and high cheekbones and a suntan that's peeling at her temples and forehead. She greets Micha like they're old friends, and she slides him a chocolate before Carter's even got both feet inside.

Temera's Ephemera's is all junk: a library of used and abused books in the storefront's right corner, many of their spines bleached from the sunlight beaming in through the windows; cast-off jewelry in a case at the store's middle; clothes on the left side, barely organized by gender, and definitely not by size. Then in the rear and on the second floor, which is really just a catwalk that looms above the back half of the store, a tumult of random thrift: Christmas decorations, old toys, battered board games, endless rows of glassware and kitchen equipment going rusty. A bevy of old CDs and vinyl records no one wants and even eight tracks and cassette tapes, VHS movies and DVDs. Some video games,

32

garbage titles that not even the most hipster gamer would deign to play. The girl's voice is perky, and she talks to Micha like an old friend. What surprises Carter, even though it shouldn't, is that Micha does the same. A part of Carter understands that only he and the rest of the Lake | Drive staff have any idea that anyone is missing, but it's still bewildering to watch Micha be all chummy with someone who is, for all intents and purposes, a perfect stranger. Carter feels a tilting in his chest and feet, as if an earthquake is uprooting the store and sliding it into a maw-shaped pit.

Micha never buys anything, which never bothered Flower. He would touch and prod, pick up and poke, always careful to return books to the proper shelves, sweaters to their hangers, toys to their bins. Sometimes Carter sucked in a breath as Micha palmed a drinking glass or a heavy pitcher, but he always put them back with delicate care, as if he was cradling a newborn or a kitten.

It's disturbing to watch the new girl act as if everything is normal. Carter pictures his brother taking his place at Lake | Drive, donning his starched white shirt with the simple black cufflinks, the non-skid shoes that don't look fashionable on anyone, not even Timothie. Carter wonders what it would be like to switch places, to spend his entire life in the oven of the yurt, to be thought of by his parents as a burden rather than a gift, practically a discarded barn animal rather than a young man. But then he watches as Micha shuffles through a display of records that he's looked at every week for the last year, his face scrunched in concentration as if this is the first time he's ever seen them. The wonder he seems to experience when he pauses on cover art that catches his eye, steals his breath, drags him off to a new world. How his fingers cascade over the sleeve as if reading the most wondrous sentences in Braille. How he then puts the record back and moves on to the next wonder, the next treasure. Maybe, Carter thinks, it wouldn't be so bad.

EVAN

WORKING at the credit union from nine to four is mostly boring, half-assed flirtation with Elena, the other teller, who wears sharp suits and pinstripe pants that suction to her ass, which is plump and buoyant and bobs with the perfect jiggle when she walks from her terminal to the break room and back. She's got midnight-indigo hair, something from a box, but it looks good on her, popping against the alabaster of her skin, which is perfectly smooth. Though she paints her nails a different color every day, she keeps her face scrubbed clean, which Evan knows not because he's really keen on that kind of observation about makeup use but because she told him so his first day.

The credit union is less noisy than Lake | Drive, and he's not forced to be nearly as demure and chummy, except for with the handful of business owners who are pals with his manager, which is weird to him because they're a bunch of Republican cowboys who love their cigars and woman-hating and want to be told, "Yes, Sir," "Of course, Sir," "Thank you, Sir," men whom Elena seems to know are showing up and suddenly needs to send bills through the counter right as they walk in, leaving them for Evan to deal with. Salazar, his manager, is nothing like them: younger, first of all, perhaps in his early thirties, and definitely not Caucasian, though he's mastered the Midwestern non-accent that business people seem to think equates to acumen officially and whiteness unofficially.

But Salazar has vanished when Evan walks into work, bleary and tired from a long night at Lake | Drive; a trio of cornball women in heavy makeup, with bright fringy highlights in their hair and wearing tight tank tops, appeared out of nowhere at ten, half an hour before closing time. Glenn was already stationed at the bar, clutching his Dewars, already on a third double because he was drinking faster than usual after Rhoda's disappearance, and the ladies persuaded him quickly to order Wendy to char them up some well-done sirloins. Doug was about to clock out, having refreshed the salad station and apportioned out hard-boiled eggs and bacon bits perfectly for the next day, but the women wanted Caesar salads sans croutons, and when Evan put in the order he marched back and offered apologies to both of them after pouring a trio of local pilsners for them when they asked for beers that were delicious but light on the carbs.

He'd stood behind the bar for another hour and a half, refilling Glenn's glass as he flirted with the women, his gallon of Dewars seeming to have erased his memory of Rhoda's disappearance, asking them if the steaks were cooked to their liking ("Oh, yes," one said, "very much so"). They'd tipped Evan nicely, a ten spot each on their split seventy-dollar check, and each had offered him a kiss on the cheek. Once they'd finally left, Glenn had wanted to shoot the shit while Evan refilled his garnishes and inventoried the well liquor. He dragged cases of bottled beer from the kitchen walk-in and restocked the refrigerators beneath the soda gun.

All this to say that, in the morning, when his alarm blares at seven-thirty, he is exhausted, having not left Lake | Drive until one-thirty. And then he's the only one to recognize that the manager is not the manager he knows. He's used to Salazar's tight suit jackets probably one size too small; they tighten at his belly, which is domed forward,

36

he likes to joke, from too much beer and too little exercise, his voice tinged with a bit of sorrow when he pats himself. Evan imagines that Sal still tries to stuff himself in clothes that fit when he was in his twenties. He's otherwise garrulous and kind, even when someone makes a serious mistake or their drawer is off by twenty bucks, which he fixes by extracting a bill from his own wallet and winking as he slides it in with the others.

But today Salazar is nowhere to be found. Instead a white-haired woman with a severe glare behind thick glasses stares at Evan as he clocks in, yawning and sipping from the cup of too-sugared coffee he picked up at the tiny drive-thru place next door to the bank, where the girl who usually hands him his order was replaced by a sleepy-looking boy who blinked and said, "Who?" when Evan asked why Summer wasn't working.

He manages not to say anything to Elena. He watches her and the two bankers who sit at their long desks, towers of paperwork on either side of them, waiting for clients to come in looking to open new accounts or apply for mortgage loans. He's never really understood how the credit union can justify employing both of them, as Thomasville is hardly a booming metropolis with new business ventures cropping up on the regular or people looking to buy new houses en masse. Mostly, the foot traffic comes stomping up to him or Elena, managers at the pizza joint or one of the clothing stores on the downtown square that primarily cater to the students, selling screen-printed t-shirts by the hundred and bulky sweaters with stitched-on letters.

Evan is glad Elena is on commercial, because he keeps not recognizing the businessmen and -women coming in with their leather zipper satchels full of rubberbanded bills that she feeds into the counting machine, chatting away with these strangers as if she's known them her whole life. Dealing with individuals who want to deposit checks or cash—Carter makes an appearance at ten-thirty with a week's worth of tip money, half of it wrinkled from spending hours in his apron pockets—is much easier, because Evan doesn't have to pretend to recognize anyone, even the people whom he does. The strange woman in the thick glasses, whom Elena refers to once as Deborah, disappears into the managerial office, and, finally, when he comes back from his lunch break, he experimentally asks Elena, "Who is that?"

She looks at him like he's a crazy person, then laughs, says, "You're funny."

Evan says nothing. Elena is distracted by the owner of the independent bookstore that competes with the one on campus. He unloads a stack of checks on her that she enters into her computer one at a time, keyboard clacking. Evan turns to look at the manager's office, all glass windows whose inner blinds are pulled up, Salazar's style, which this Deborah woman appears to be imitating. She is sitting at the computer, leaning toward the monitor, lips pursed. Though she appears puzzled by whatever she's reading (she scribbles something on a legal pad, then clicks around, arm twitching as it guides the mouse), she seems comfortable. As if she's been there forever.

Evan clocks out at four, practically changing his clothes while he drives home, loosening his tie with one hand while he steers with the other. He kicks off his loafers into the driver-side wheel well, depressing the gas and brake with his socked foot. He has less than an hour to get to Lake | Drive. His apartment is on the south side of Thomasville, past the college tennis courts and ROTC climbing walls. Most students live north of campus in the residential grid of low-slung bungalows with tilting front porches and crappy kitchens and backyards the size of kiddie pools. Evan's studio is a room above the detached garage of a math professor's house, which he rents to Evan for next to nothing. In return, Evan mows the yard twice a month and waters his plants when the professor goes out of town for conferences. The drive from the credit union takes ten minutes not because it's a long distance—nothing in Thomasville is far from anything else, except for the Walmart on the northern end of town—but because of the endless army of stop signs and blinking red lights and the twenty-five miles per hour speed limit.

Thankfully, the math professor didn't vanish; he's out in the front yard when Evan pulls into the driveway, down on his knees in front of the flower beds that line the house, trimming his gladiolas. The professor never asks Evan to handle any of the landscaping besides the grass, for which Evan is grateful.

The professor is the only person who knows Evan's secret: that he's dropped out of school.

He wasn't doing poorly. In fact, during the spring semester he earned a 4.0. Evan just hated school. He'd only enrolled because that's what his family did: his three older siblings went to Iowa, Dartmouth, and UC-Riverside, respectively, all desperate to flock away from St. Louis, something else that hadn't interested Evan much. His parents were both PhDs, his mother in English and his father in chemistry, even though neither was working in the academy (she was a technical writer for a pharmaceutical company and he had joined an upstart manufacturing company as an engineer, doing who knows what), and they'd both bonked around the country for their various degrees before settling in the Midwest when his father landed his first job at Boeing. Evan, who had spent high school clearing through honors courses without sweating even the big research papers for his AP English and History classes, had applied only to McClain State, which had offered him a gargantuan scholarship that included enough money to study abroad one semester in his junior or senior year.

But he hated being a student. No matter the subject—marketing, creative writing, art history, even a class on *Star Wars*, films he'd grown up watching over and over—being stuck in an uncomfortable desk, listening to a professor drawl on and on (or, in the case of instructors who weren't in love with the sound of their own voices, having to hear his classmates feign interest in a topic) left him emotionally stultified. He would start falling asleep even if he wasn't tired, and he was called out by a teacher more than once for slumping over, eyes closed, in the middle of some explainer on Roman architecture or the declension of French nouns. Evan tried, he really did, to find something that mattered to him, a subject that would engross him enough to spend three hours each week in a classroom and endless more time reading textbooks or articles, but nothing doing. When he finally decided, at the end of his junior year, not to register for fall classes, he instead found extra work at the credit union—he was already bartending at Lake | Drive most nights—and opted not to tell anyone about his changed trajectory.

The professor, his back turned, lifts a hand and waves. Evan clomps up the stairs—strong, new, painted white—that wrap up the side of the garage and unlocks his apartment door.

Evan isn't big on décor, and someone seeing his apartment for the first time might laugh. Timothie, the one time they hooked up, said, "Holy shit, it's the stereotypical bachelor pad. Are you divorced or something?"

His only furniture is a card table in the kitchenette, a rickety red futon too short for a grown person to lie down on, a claptrap coffee table made of particle board, and his bed, the box spring set directly on the floor. His alarm clock sits on the ground, too, mostly because that way Evan has to make too much effort in the mornings to shut it off and go back to sleep. The walls are largely blank, and he has only three light sources: the two overheads—one above the bed in the sleeping nook, another above the stove—and a goosenecked lamp next to the futon. The floors are some kind of scuffed vinyl meant to look like gray wood. The air is always stifling, not exactly hot but heavy, as if the place has been cinched up for months every time Evan walks in.

Lake | Drive is chaos when he arrives. There's confusion at the host stand, where a party of twelve is convinced that they've successfully made a 4:30 reservation for the bump-out room, even though every employee knows that those tables can't be claimed until six pm or later; no one is sure who has given the party's organizer, a man in his sixties with an orange-glow tan and stalks of silver hair that are slicked into spikes like something from the early 2000s, who demands to speak to a manager every five minutes while Perry tries to assuage him, staring at his reservation book as though the answers will suddenly appear out of nowhere. But Glenn is having his own rampage through the kitchen, not because one of the cooks has fucked something up—besides the wayward twelve-top, there's only one other table in the dining room, and their tempeh bowls have already been delivered no problem—but because his entire extended family is acting as though Rhoda doesn't exist; no one seems worried about her, and when Glenn called the police, they apparently claimed there's no record of her birth, no driver's license, not even a marriage license on file.

And then there's Doug, who, as he finishes prepping his station for the night, wiping down his cutting board and scrubbing away juice spilled by freshly-sliced heirloom tomatoes, is bopping with a cartoon-ish energy. When he sees Evan clocking in, he lights up, throws down his soiled rag, and rushes over. He clutches Evan's arm and, without any preamble, says, "You'll never believe it. I did it."

Evan looks him over. Doug looks like he's on speed. "Did what?"

"I made someone remember. Evan, I made someone remember the people who are gone."

SCOTT

IT'S clear that Glenn is really is losing it when he asks Scott if he'll stick around when Evan arrives, not to serve as a backup bartender but to work The Drive.

"Why me?" Scott says.

Glenn, red-eyed, too much red scruff grown across his neck and down his chin, plops down on one of the bar stools. "Why the fuck not you?"

"I've never done it. I've never even worked the bump-out."

"Fuck the bump-out," Glenn growls, waving for a Dewars. Scott pours. "Fuck 'never'. You'll make easy money."

"Okay," Scott says. "I guess."

And so he finds himself, at six-thirty, on the back of a golf cart while Satiya drives. The Drive is a quarter of a mile down the narrow asphalt walking path that skirts the edge of Thomasville lake, counter-clockwise from the restaurant. Two gazebos stand next to each other, one dressed out with an outdoor kitchen that generates power from god-knows-where and the other home to a single table that can be set for anywhere between two and six people, rounded leaves hooked to the undersides for easy expansion. In the kitchen gazebo, the gas stove has already been lit, the oven is preheated, and the refrigerator is stocked with chilled white wine and bottles of water. If tonight's guests—a three-top, including the McClain president and some bigwig from some accrediting body—want anything else to drink, Scott will zip back to the restaurant in the golf cart. Satiya will deliver the guests in fifteen minutes, which she tells Scott right before she zips away, leaving him to set the table.

It's a perfect night for outdoor eating; the temperature has taken a balmy plunge into the low seventies, and the humidity is broken, thanks to a mid-day rain shower. Scott would prefer to be getting ready for a night out at the bars, which is really just a goofy lap around the downtown square with diversions down a few side streets to the dives with decent drink specials, especially in the summer when they're desperate for business and compete with one another over who can come closest to their bottom line. But at least the view is good, the water of the lake clear and smelling, for once, more like the ocean than a morgue. He gets to work quickly; in the kitchen gazebo is a stainless steel cabinet, like something you would see in a warehouse or office mail room. Scott finds tablecloths wrapped in plastic, along with pre-rolled sets of silverware in the ubiquitous peach Lake | Drive napkins. He snags three sets and combats an obnoxious breeze as he lays out the tablecloth. He wipes stray leaves and a few husked acorns from the chairs and sweeps out the entire gazebo with the broom he finds next to the cabinet. Stemware waits next to the stovetop, the glass warmed by the burners whose gas rings flicker in the wind. He hears the roar of the golf cart as he's finishing, flicking away a lightning bug that alights on the white tablecloth. He stands outside the gazebo, hands behind his back, and watches the guests—two men in their fifties or sixties and a much younger woman—clamber out of the golf cart, looking windblown but gleeful at the expensive, fanciful scene. Scott has managed, just in time, to extract life from the LED candles he found in the lowest cabinet, smacking their bottoms to get the triple-A batteries to do their job.

"Well, look at this," one of the men says. He's bald except for a wispy crown of brown hair streaked with gray circumnavigating his head like a laurel wreath. "Enchanting." He smiles and winks at Scott, who simply nods, tilting his entire body forward just so. The other two diners cling to one another as if they're marching through a snowstorm even though the breeze has died down. The woman's high heels clip-clop against the asphalt and the three wooden steps leading into the gazebo.

"This is Scott," Satiya says. She's donned her white chef's coat, which blares against her olive skin. She's all long nose and wide brown eyes. "He'll be taking care of you this evening." She explains the drink situation and runs through the menu, then leaves to begin prepping the salads and searing the ahi for the appetizer. Once seated, his guests stare at him.

"Good evening," he says, voice even. Scott knows how to change his timbre and tone, even how to lower his shoulders so they're more rounded—a former swimmer, he knows he's broad, possibly imposing to the wrong guests—and thus making him appear more docile. He's quick to study facial expressions, good at seeing the way other people see him. The balding man gives him an appraising look, the slightest nod of approval, a glance toward his dinner companions. Scott stands up straighter, sucks in his non-existent gut, and asks what they would each like to drink.

Dinner goes smoothly. The balding man is a representative from the Higher Learning Commission. Scott figures out that the young woman's name is Marissa, and she is the daughter of the second man, who is, in fact, the McClain State President. His hair black and thick, his mouth etched with lines when he talks, lines that grow deeper and more numerous when he smiles, which is a lot. He drinks his wine slowly, taking big but infrequent sips. Marissa pulls the bottle from its marble cooling sleeve frequently, and she meets Scott's eyes whenever she's ready for him to bring another. If either her father or the commissioner notices they're on their third bottle, at least one and a half of them tucked away in Marissa's gullet, neither shows it.

They ooh and ahh over the food, and when they've had enough to drink, they start calling out their gratitude to Satiya, voices carrying across the warm wind. She raises a hand in acknowledgement every time, her body shimmying as she sautés asparagus and sears their steaks, which they've each ordered medium rare. As far as dinner parties go, they're not needy; each takes a normal-sized helping of black peppercorns and shaved parmigiana on their Caesar salads. They polish off their ahi appetizer, which make the president moan and lick his fingers unapologetically. None of them request steak sauce when the entrees arrive, but as Scott is removing their plates the president asks for a list of scotches, and Scott manages to rattle off most of what's behind the bar back at the restaurant: Dewars, of course, Glenfiddich, Balvenie, Macallan, Lagavulin. The president holds up a hand eventually and says, "Three Laphroaigs," to which Marissa and the rep offer no objections. When Scott explains that he'll have to return to the restaurant, they nod agreeably. He takes the keys to the golf cart from Satiya, who is busy bruleeing the tops of three slices of cheesecake.

Rather than pour the Laphroaigs into rocks glasses and worry about them sloshing across the leatherette seats of the golf cart as he careens around the lake, Scott slips into the restaurant and steals the bottle, leaving a note for Evan, who is somewhere in the kitchen helping run food. The dining room is jammed, and Scott can see parties milling at the front despite the fact that it's well past eight. Perry is pretending to pore over the floor chart, as if he can will empty tables into existence

46

with his stare. Timothie and Rion, Andre and Andrew, Donny and Carter, are all rushing around, check booklets perched in their aprons, condiments speared between fingers, trays of steaming dishes held high. The busboys rush to clear empty tables, their tubs full of stemware and dirtied plates. Scott hears the churn of the ice machine, the screech of Merebeth yelling for something to be cooked on the fly. He takes the bottle by the throat and slips past Timothie, who comes rocketing out of the kitchen with a pair of dinner salads in his hands.

Because of the scrum and chaos, he doesn't get a chance to speak to Doug, who is too busy prepping a chef salad and then a Waldorf and then a wilted and then a steak-and-greens to talk to anyone. But Scott will learn, when the night is over, the revelation that he's missed. That, before Lake | Drive was rocked by an unexpectedly heavy dinner rush two days after the disappearances that only its staff notices, Doug managed to bring someone's memory back. And he became convinced that each and every one of them could do it, too.

PART TWO

YOU

YOU *cannot help but smile.*

You watch them discover, disentangle, distort. Deny, discuss, decide.

They do not wonder what you might know. They cannot tell that your hands are the ones that have done this, that have rewoven the fabric of their world, leaving their minds in tune, their memories intact.

You watch them, the disturbed world at their feet, the choices, the chances, the changes, the challenges. You feast on these as if every moment is a nourishing scoop of ambrosial delight.

The world needed to be different, and it is so.

And now you watch, a swelling in your chest at each change, each shift. Each choice.

MEREBETH

MEREBETH'S hands are blistered and cut and bruised and broken and scraped and burned. But that's how life is for a cook, flaying steaks and searing chicken and slicing potatoes that spill out steam like exhaled breath. Fingering hot tongs, handling sharp knives whose edges glint under hard kitchen light.

Doug will not stop talking.

She likes him well enough. She thinks it's cruel, Glenn keeping him stuck at the salad station while the other boys, those boys who are beautiful, young, strong, and sometimes smart, sometimes dumber than canvas sacks, run around the dining room and flirt with one another. She knows that Doug yearns to be with them, among them, wearing the same clean starched shirts and pants, chatting up tables, taking home stacks of cash, bitching about the bad tippers. Instead, he's stuck digging through heaps of Romaine to find weevils and other insects before they end up on someone's salad plate. He's stuck ladling out dressings and cutting croutons, breaking down endless supplies of tomatoes and green peppers and hard-boiled eggs. And being the only boy in the kitchen, well; that's just extra cruelty. The women of the kitchen treat him well enough, even if Cynthia does "accidentally" spray him with the hose when he brings a drained tin of ranch dressing over to the dish station. And then there's Wendy, who likes to talk loudly about her menstrual cycle when he's within shouting distance just to make him blush. Merebeth still remembers her last boyfriend being shocked when she explained, calmly, that she did not bleed from the same place she peed.

She's only half-listening to Doug at first, who started and is now ending his shift dithering about the disappearances. He hasn't stopped talking about them for days, though she can't really blame him. It's fair to be freaked out; she certainly was when she discovered that her next-door neighbors had been replaced. They were a lovely African American couple who were always leaving banana bread on her stoop, wrapped up tight in aluminum foil with a beautiful calligraphied note tied on with red ribbon, her name written in swooping letters, miraculously spelled correctly every time. Now she's stuck with some loud white guy who wears wife beaters that show off his stooped, shaggy shoulders and his equally hirsute beer gut. He's been working on a run-down truck more rust than paint, the hood popped open and half of its innards scattered about on the driveway, a boom box in the grass blasting nonsense rap music. She hasn't made any effort to introduce herself, and when she said so, her wife, Amy, looked puzzled.

"Introduce yourself to who?" she said.

"The weird guy next door."

"Phil? He's not weird."

"You know him?"

Amy looked at her like Merebeth was speaking in tongues. "He's lived here longer than we have."

Right, Merebeth thought.

She manages to tune in just in time for Doug's big reveal: that he made his roommate become aware of the disappearances.

She's arranging some frites next to a well-done steak, the last ticket on the wheel. Timothie is leaning against the ice machine, scrolling through his phone. Angela enters the kitchen and rolls her eyes at him. Glenn has long had a policy against phone use while on the clock, but since his wife vanished he's not noticed anything, at least not with the boys. Yesterday he chewed Merebeth out over not seeing that a ticket required a side of steamed broccoli rather than the fries she'd piled next to a wagyu burger. An easy fix; the fries didn't even have to get tossed out. But Glenn screeched about overhead anyway. She wanted to slap him with her grease-slicked spatula.

"Hang on," she says, sliding the steak and frites into the expo window and pulling down the ticket. She slips it beneath the plate and yells, "Order up," even though Timothie is already pocketing his phone. She turns back to Doug. "What are you talking about?"

Doug sighs but doesn't roll his eyes. He's diminutive, the shortest guy that works in the restaurant. He reminds her of Diego Schwartzman, her favorite tennis player not because he's earned any of the accolades that Federer or Nadal or—gross—Djokovic have stacked up next to their names but because, for all his tiny stature, he's managed to carve out a career for himself. He stands tall among giants. Merebeth has always thought of herself as a returner rather than someone who starts on offense. It doesn't help in most kitchens, waiting for someone to dig at you rather than doing the digging first, but here at Lake | Drive women rule the roost. Or at least the flattop.

"I made my roommate remember." Doug blinks and turns back to the salad station, where he busies himself scrubbing away the detritus of so many onionskins leeched into the cutting board.

"Hang on," Merebeth says. She softens her voice. "How did you do that?"

Doug turns back to her. His eyes are lidded, like he's convinced she's going to make fun of him for whatever he says.

"Really," she says. "I want to know."

Angela, who is still lurking at the expo line, filling plastic ramekins full of sour cream, pauses to watch their exchange, which strikes Merebeth as odd. Angela, despite her clear status as Glenn's favorite—regardless of what Timothie thinks—never looks at Merebeth, which is fine, because Merebeth hardly thinks of Angela at all, even if she is gorgeous: all legs and long hair. Looks a little—really, a lot—like Amy.

Doug sets down his rag, soaked with sanitizer and degreaser, and leans against the station counter. "I don't know," he says. "Really. I just touched his arm and said something like, 'Don't you remember?' And then he did."

"And that was it?"

"He freaked out for a while. I had to sit him down and explain. I thought he might pass out."

"I see."

"He's fine now. At least, as far as I know. He could be dead." When he sees the soured look on Merebeth's face, he holds up his hands in defense. "I'm kidding. At least I hope so. I doubt he's dead. Maybe still confused?"

"There's plenty to be confused about," Merebeth says.

She's quick to clean up her line, taking inventory of how many pickled onions and cornichons are left. She counts the sirloins and makes a note that the supply of sliced shiitakes is low. She and Cynthia drag the fryers out to the grease disposal and, grunting, manage to drain them without spilling too much on their shoes and pants. By the time Merebeth clocks out, it's after midnight.

Merebeth is often delirious with exhaustion on these drives home, the lakeside dark, the trees lining the state highway looming in her headlights. Usually she blasts the air conditioning, even in winter, the sting of cold air keeping her awake long enough to reach the house and tumble into bed without showering, Amy already tucked up under the covers no matter the weather, turned on her side toward the window, back to Merebeth not because she's pissed at her wife's late hours—she has long understood what it means to be married to someone in the restaurant business—but because that's how her body naturally flops and turns in slumber. Merebeth, not the sort to read into things, has long accepted this explanation.

But tonight, Merebeth is wired, thanks to Doug's story. She pictures herself entering through the kitchen door, not bothering to keep the noise down because she plans to wake Amy anyway. She'll clutch her wife's wrists and look her in the eyes and say, "I need you to remember," or "Do you know that people disappeared? That they've been replaced?" Maybe she'll add, "Fuck that weirdo Phil," and something will come over Amy, her wide eyes going sleepy—sleepier—and then something will jolt through her and she will know, she will cry out about the missing neighbors and their delicious banana bread. Merebeth will show her that the wrong man is president and Amy will agree, she will curse and scream, and then when Merebeth starts crying with joy Amy will hold her tight, the pliant softness of Amy's back and shoulders like a pillow, and she will let Merebeth sob out her joy, all of her concern and fear and sorrow whisked away by tears, sorrow and fear because she couldn't imagine living the rest of her life in a world so different from the one Amy knows, remembering things and people that Amy doesn't. As her crying subsides Amy will kiss her neck, the tender place beneath her right ear that they both know makes Merebeth wet, and then they will slide hands up one another's shirts, Merebeth laughing as she tries to meander her way beneath Amy's nightgown, a ridiculous lime green thing that only an old lady should be wearing, a joke between them but annoying in this moment, requiring Amy to simply tear the thing off, which is fine because they're headed for sex anyway, wetness and fingers and tongues and heavy breathing. And when they're both satisfied they will lie together atop the duvet, breathing as one, Amy asking Merebeth to explain how she did what she did and why the disappearances happened and why she remembered but Amy did not and Merebeth will say, "I don't know," voice still a bit cragged and gummy, and even though she'll offer nothing of substance Amy will nod, hair clinging to the pillowcase, and she will fall asleep before Merebeth, who will come along shortly thereafter into dreams, pleasant and wispy and quick to vanish in the morning, when they will eat eggs and drink coffee and simply be, together, figuring out all of the ways that the world has changed. It will be, Merebeth decides as she pulls into the driveway, a game, because how else can one manage to get through this weird new existence otherwise?

She steps out of her car. The night is crisp.

She goes inside, the house dark.

And everything unfolds exactly as she hopes.

SATIYA

AS soon as word gets out about what Merebeth has done—no one listens to poor Doug, but they listen to her—Satiya decides to drive home. She'll spend the three hours from Thomasville to St. Peters figuring out which of her parents, mother or father, she should awaken.

No one else has used that word, but it's the first thing that came into her head when Merebeth, barging into the kitchen, told everyone about Amy.

Satiya has experienced lots of awakenings.

First: seventh grade science class. Until then, she'd been convinced she would become a doctor, like her mother who ran a successful OB/GYN clinic in a hospital, where she specialized in neonatal. Her nurses loved her. Satiya had spent many a weekend while her father—an account executive for an advertising firm in St. Louis—jetted off to conferences and weekend-long luncheons with New York clients that for some reason wanted their commercials scripted and blocked by a Midwestern company. She'd watched her mother rove from room to room, her voice soothing and sweet, almost like she was singing to the pregnant women, her nursing staff her backup singers, checking vitals, providing ice chips, helping with breathing exercises during contractions. But then Satiya saw the dead frog in a dissection pan and, when she picked up the scalpel, sure she would have no trouble slicing through the rubbery body, her limbs emptied. Her head felt like it was swelling to three times its normal size. She nearly vomited, and perspiration lined her forehead with such stinky thickness she may as well have been caught in a rainstorm. Her partner, a girl named Breanne who would go on to be a soccer star at UNC, grabbed the scalpel from her hand and pushed her onto her stool, where she sat, bewildered and nauseous, until class was over. She knew, then, that she couldn't be a doctor. Instead, she would be an artist.

Then, awakening number two: sophomore year at McClain. After the disaster with the frog—and several subsequent disasters involving a sheep's eye and a cow's brain; she barely scored a B in science that year—she'd thrown herself into drawing, knowing she wasn't great at it but knew—thought, at least—that she could get better. And she did, all throughout high school, where she took an art class every year even though the one full-time faculty member in the department was a sleepy woman who would lecture for fifteen minutes once a week and then send everyone loose to paint or sketch or even use the firing kiln to make limp, uneven coffee cups. Satiya studied the methods and work of Paul Cadden, Zaha Hadid, Henry Moore, and Hector Gonzales. She watched endless YouTube tutorials, and finally, as a junior, she was able to get human eyes and noses right. She transitioned to acrylics, which she thought she would love, and at first she did. Mixing colors on a palette, applying gesso to a blank canvas: she loved imagining the endless possibilities, the shapes and textures that could be made with a good hog's hairbrush. But it turned out that she was a better thinker than painter. She was competent enough; that was the word used more than once by her Painting I and II professor, a stout bald man who stood at the front of the studio with his beefy arms crossed over his chest, tight black t-shirt pulling at his shoulders, and explained technique as though he was reading from a user's manual for a lawnmower.

He would stalk the room, pausing at each student's work-in-progress, and nod, then shake his head and mutter to himself, leaving the artist unsure of whether they were doing things right or wrong. Satiya was never doing either; she was just doing, if the way she meagerly passed her portfolio review—hardly any comments from the trio of professors reviewing each student except, again, that word "competent" written in a comment box all lonely and aloof—was any indication. She powered through, but at the end of her junior year she decided to find a part-time job even though she didn't really need the money and she had little free time, considering her studio courses gobbled up so many hours in a day for so few credits. Where her English and History major friends really did only spend three hours a week in their seminars and lectures, she was mired in six-hours-a-week courses that left her with pain in her lower back and smudges of paint and clay embedded under her fingernails. She found work at Lake | Drive when Ethan, whom she sat next to in a business class she was taking as an elective for reasons she couldn't articulate, told her that one of the line cooks had quit and his boss was desperate for a hard worker to replace her. Satiya, who had little to no cooking experience, took the gig, lying her way through the brief interview that took place at the restaurant bar at three in the afternoon, Scott—whose name she didn't know yet—smirking at her while he pretended to wash out pint glasses. If Glenn couldn't see through her fabricated work experience, he sure did. But he didn't say anything.

Third awakening: she loved to cook. It became a sort of art. Even something as simple as a platter of fried things, chicken wings or frites or mushrooms, could catch the light at a certain angle to make them look more appealing, browned surfaces glistening with oil. The sear of steaks, the shape of a heap of mashed potatoes with gravy drizzled over the mound, roasted salsify sprinkled with garlic and parsley so that the seasonings flashed and dotted the root like constellations. And dessert! Sliced lemon meringues with carefully decorative scorching from the cooking torch, intricate latticework on raspberry and blackberry pies, heaps of ice cream stacked next to a volcanic, oozing chocolate three-layer cake. Baking was more complicated, the directions more precise, measurements of flour and butter and salt not allowing for as many extremes of experimentation, but Satiya still found joy in the whirls and flourishes on chocolate tarts and berry crepes. Glenn and Merebeth eventually agreed to give her free range, establishing a new dessert menu every few days depending on what she felt like designing and whatever ingredients she could scrounge from the walk-in. When she graduated from McClain, she didn't bother leaving Thomasville or looking for work in an art gallery or museum, nor did she even remotely consider moving on to an MFA or design school. Instead, she stuck with Lake | Drive, feeling more like an artist than ever. Her parents weren't happy, she could tell, but they didn't try to persuade her to move home; the money was good, especially for somewhere with cheap rent like Thomasville, even though she was three hours away from her mother and father and worked six days a week, Sundays her only bit of respite.

Three major awakenings. And now, she will try to offer a fourth, but to someone else.

Traffic is light, so she's able to coast at a reasonable seventy-five down highway 63, the four lanes generally clear of traffic; if she comes upon a slow driver, she has plenty of space to move into the left lane and back without slowing down. Cars snarl up the exit for interstate 70, Mizzou students and the Columbia brunch crowd clogging the highway overpass, but aside from that, she makes good time. Satiya doesn't need to stop for gas or bathroom breaks—she's judicious with the bottle of water sitting in her cupholder—and so this gives her tons of uninterrupted time to think about what she will do.

She loves her parents equally. Amah, her mother, cooked and baked for her and sewed up her beloved clothes whenever they tore, washing them vigorously if they were stained, singing her to sleep when she was terrified of the dark or suffering heartache at the hands of a stupid adolescent boy she thought she loved. Her father, Patrick, always made time for her despite his busy schedule, bringing her gifts from his trips around the country even when she was too old to need or expect such trinkets. They've both given her everything that parents could give. They even sent her money every month all throughout her four undergraduate years, a stipend of sorts so that she didn't have to worry about working. She didn't tell them about Lake | Drive until she had to explain why she wasn't moving back to the area or off to some new adventurous clime after graduation, an admission that Patrick had barely hidden his disappointment in, his voice cracking as he said, "Oh," and then, "Well, I want you to do what makes you happy, Sati."

How to choose who should know that the world has changed? She flip-flops each mile: first to her mother, whose family didn't want her to become a doctor, which always felt strange to Satiya, because wasn't that one of the stereotypes about Indians who send their children to study in the United States? The way Amah told it, her parents had wanted her to catch a rich white man—which, Satiya supposes, she did—and raise half-a-dozen children; her side of the family was gargantuan, too many aunts and uncles and cousins for Satiya to keep track of. It would make sense to awaken her mother, because the odds are greater that some of them have vanished. At the same time, wouldn't knowing that people are missing be more painful than not? Could blissful ignorance be superior?

And then there's her father, his own family long dead. She hasn't

62

asked many questions about what happened to her paternal grandparents, who were killed in some kind of accident well before Satiya was born, a tragedy that is partly responsible for her father's wealth: life insurance policies were cashed for him when he was barely in college, and instead of blowing the dough on beer and drugs and cars or whatever, he stashed it away in an investment account that ballooned as he graduated and found work coming up with jingles and commercial concepts. He had no siblings, and so it's hard to fathom who he might want to know is gone. But what about co-workers, or friends—he goes out golfing on weekends with a rotating cast of college fraternity brothers when he's not aflight—that are missing from his life? But then the same thing: would knowing that things are different and wrong, and being the only one who knows it, make life better or worse?

She still hasn't decided when she pulls into her parents' subdivision. The entrance is bordered by swooping brickwork that resembles a pair of inverted culverts, each with affixed gold lettering: the one on the left reads *Carmine* and the one on the right *Estates*. The houses are all two-stories with brick exteriors, generous lawns, two- and three-car garages, Corinthian columns holding up decorative balconies. The architecture is largely repetitive, every house adorned with the same shutters pinned to the brick, the same bay window bulging from each living room, the same double front doors opening into the same foyer. The neighborhood is idyllic if a bit *Stepford Wives* for Satiya's taste, and she doesn't like talk of how it's a "good" part of town. St. Peters is all white-flight, all conservative, all upper middle class people who vote for the people who say they won't increase taxes and hate abortion. No one here drives an electric car, because they don't think about things like the environment except when rain threatens birthday parties and Fourth of July barbecues. The schools are all very good.

63

Even though Satiya hasn't called to let her parents know she's coming, her mother flings open the front door before she's fully out of her car, which she parks along the curb beneath the reaching branches of a giant oak tree whose leaves are a verdant green. The landscaping company that mows the grass has been by recently if the perfect lines of directional trim are any evidence. Certainly her father doesn't have time for that kind of labor, and while her mother loves the peonies and milkweed that line the front walk, she has the exact opposite of a green thumb; every time Amah buys plants and waters them herself, they die.

Amah cuts through the grass, barefoot, and grabs Satiya up in a hug. Her mother smells of lavender and lilacs, powerful perfumes and body lotions she slathers on her hands to keep them soft; she claims that this is for the sake of patients, citing the need for a comforting touch when pressing a cold stethoscope to a breastbone or palpitating an abdomen, but Satiya knows that it's really part of the endless urge to feel and look youthful. Her mother is in her early fifties, crows' feet just starting to crowd around her almond-shaped eyes, gray filaments dazzled through her licorice-black hair that falls in a single thick twist around the right side of her throat and drapes across her breast. It tickles Satiya's nose as her mother squeezes. Amah has always been a specimen of miraculous physical shape, the long hours at her private practice not stopping her from taking Zumba classes at night and doing push-ups and sit-ups in the morning like she's enlisted in the military. Patrick jokes that she has better abs than he does.

"What are you doing here?" Amah says when she releases Satiya. She's beaming, but then she frowns. "Is everything okay?"

"Everything's fine," Satiya says, her heart beating fast. "It's my day off. I thought I'd surprise you."

"Well, your father isn't home yet. He's in Albuquerque doing some-

64

thing or other. He won't be back until this evening."

Satiya nods, but she roils. It's possible the decision, then, has been made for her.

She follows her mother inside. As they walk through the entryway, she peers at all the family photos mounted on the wall: everyone looks to be in place. The day after the disappearances, Satiya sat down on her sofa and scrolled through her cell phone, checking her contacts, her texts, her photos. Two friends from undergrad had vanished entirely; a dozen photographs that she'd saved on her cell had disappeared. So Satiya is careful to take stock of every piece of possible evidence she can of sudden absence from her parents' life, but as Amah instructs her to sit down at the kitchen table so she can boil them both some oolong tea—Satiya's favorite—she sees nothing amiss. All of the knickknacks her mother has been gifted by her book club and ladies' lunch group remain where they should be. Every photo is as she remembers it, every body captured on film a face that's at least vaguely familiar.

As has been her ritual since Satiya was a child, Amah is silent while the water in her tea kettle, saffron-gold, metal, with an elegant, delicate spout that reminds Satiya of an elephant's curved trunk, comes to a boil. Her mother stands with her back to the burner but keeps her eyes aimed toward the ceiling, and if Satiya didn't know Amah, she'd think she was praying. Her gaze is far away, as if she can see through the vaulted ceiling and the roof to the clouds, to the stars and galaxies beyond them. Satiya has wondered many times what her mother thinks about during these minutes of waiting, but she has never asked; we all have our own private worlds that we need to inhabit from time to time. We all have our tender places that shouldn't be invaded. As her parents didn't press when she abandoned medicine, and then abandoned art, she has never pressed her mother to explain what is cranking through

65

her head as she waits meditatively for the water to boil.

When the kettle screams out, her mother comes back to life, turning with languid grace to pull the water from the heat. Satiya watches as she plucks the kettle by the handle, setting it on a cold coil, and then gathers a matching pair of bone China mugs and saucers from a cabinet. She pulls loose tea from a jar on the counter and two tea infuser balls on short chains that she packs full, the woodsy, rich smell of oolong filling the kitchen. Amah plunks the balls into the empty cups and sets one in front of Satiya and the other before her own chair, then picks up the kettle and pours. Her movements are like those of someone playing a musical instrument, careful and symphonic.

Her mother sits and, while the tea steeps, asks Satiya how things are in Thomasville. It would be easy enough to read disdain or disinterest in her mother's question; she could be perceived as cavalier and off-hand as an acquaintance talking about the weather, but there's a rich integrity in Amah's voice. She looks Satiya in the eye, domes her hands together in front of her and leans forward, absorbed by Satiya's response, which she knows is lackluster: life in Thomasville is repetition, days and nights spent at Lake | Drive and little else. Satiya has never been much for socializing—beyond the jawing and laughter of the kitchen, which it took Satiya a long time to integrate herself into— and her mother knows this. So, when Satiya redirects the conversation to her mother's life, Amah either doesn't register or pretends not to notice the volley.

"We're reading some god-awful memoir for book club," Amah says, flailing a hand in the air like she's swatting a fly. "It's six hundred pages of big paragraphs and tiny font and a lot of woe-is-me-look-how-bad-my-life-as-a-moderately-middle-class-white-woman-is. Seriously, the greatest challenge this woman faced as a child was her mother accidentally selling her favorite teddy bear at a garage sale. Everyone's gone gaga over this book simply because the woman knows how to describe things using more than primary colors."

"Sounds horrible. Why not just stop reading?"

Amah tuts. "You know I always do the reading."

Satiya smiles. "I know you do." She sips her tea, which is hot but drinkable. The smell loosens something in her bones. "And how's Anlusia?"

A puzzled look crosses her mother's face, and Satiya realizes her mistake right away. She sets down her tea cup, feeling light-headed even before Amah says, "Who?"

Anlusia has been her mother's best friend for years, ever since medical school. Unlike Amah, who stayed in Missouri after they graduated from Wash U, Anlusia moved all the way to California to work as a plastic surgeon. She wasn't the type of friend her mother kept photographic evidence of around the house; for birthdays and Christmas they sent one another expensive bottles of wine or gift cards to massage therapists and day spas rather than hand-carved statuettes of birds or saints a la the book club ladies who went for kitsch when it came time for their annual Secret Santa gift exchange. The correspondence between Amah and Anlusia was delivered via letters on thick, fancy cardstock that her mother kept in a desk drawer in her office.

The stories Amah had told Satiya about Anlusia were so thorough and rich that she was practically an aunt, even though she'd only seen the woman one time in person, when Satiya was thirteen and Anlusia visited over the holidays. She stayed in the spare bedroom and was all blazing red hair and equally fiery makeup, her lips stained an almost-neon orange, her eyeshadow electric popsicle blue. She wore gargantuan press-on nails that matched her mouth, and when Satiya stared at them, Anlusia laughed and said, "Don't worry. I don't wear them when I'm doing rhinoplasties." Satiya had simply nodded. After Christmas, Anlusia had sent her a set in the mail. She'd never had the gumption to wear them, imagining how hard it would be to pick up a graphite pencil or one of her paintbrushes with those fangs attached to her fingers. Her mother was always laughing with Anlusia on the phone, recounting nights after exams when they would get plowed on cheap wine and prowl the bars in Soulard or the Central West End, undergraduate men trying to get in their pants via shots of cheap, fruity alcohol or overpriced bottles of crappy American beer. There was the time, as they walked from one bar to another in the Landing, when a man tried to steal Amah's purse and Anlusia bashed him over the head with her own gargantuan Gucci knockoff, clobbering him so hard that he fell to the ground moaning, begging her to stop pummeling him, and she hocked up a loogie that spattered across the man's cheek. The women didn't bother calling the police, laughing and hooking their arms together and leaving him to groan and wallow as they slipped into their destination and ordered celebratory cosmopolitans.

She is such an important piece of who her mother became. As such, she is a key part of who Satiya has become. They are all links in the same chain. And now she is missing from her mother's memory.

So it is easy for Satiya to reach across the table, catching her teacup with her elbow and nearly sending the oolong spilling across the surface, and curl her fingers around her mother's wrist. She can feel her mother's pulse. She hardly thinks about it as she says, "You remember Anlusia," and then, in a flash, her mother does.

W E N D Y

WENDY'S decision is easy, because she can count on one hand who in her life is important enough to give the gift of recovered memory. Unlike Satiya, she doesn't have a pair of loving parents to hem and haw over; she's not married—God, no—like Merebeth, though that seems to have made her choice easy.

Wendy chooses her sister.

She and Carla both live in town, but in separate apartments. They're the kind of siblings that love one another but would drive each other insane if they lived in the same place, as evidenced by the fact that they hated each other all throughout high school, the simplest disagreements like who would shower first in the morning setting off what seemed to be nuclear war in their house. They couldn't even settle on who sat where at dinner, especially in summer, because certain chairs at the dining room table would be bathed in hot early evening light throughout the meal. Their bickering drove their parents crazy and may have even been part of the reason they split up when Wendy left for college in Columbia a year after Carla set out for Ames.

That distance, though, brought them closer. Carla was the first to reach out, calling Wendy during her first weekend at Iowa State, sobbing that she was lonely. Her roommate, a stranger from Des Moines, had abandoned her to go to a fraternity party to which she didn't bother inviting Carla, and all of the kids she'd been friends with in high school who had chosen to become Cyclones had disappeared. Carla had no idea what to do. Instead of offering solutions or decrying her sister's pathetic breakdown, Wendy listened, which was so clearly what Carla wanted. This set off weekly calls, every weekend like clockwork, for which Wendy constantly rearranged her social calendar. Over time, the wounds that she and Carla had cut into one another seemed to heal, even though they managed to rip open over long breaks at winter and summer when they were under the same roof again. Eventually, they both started staying on their respective campuses when these rests came around, until they serendipitously both found work back home in Thomasville, Wendy at Lake | Drive, Carla in the human resources office at McClain State.

Midway through Wendy's sophomore year of college their father moved out to California to become a demented, middle-aged surfer on the weekends and to do something in finance during the week; neither Carla nor Wendy really speak to him anymore, even though the divorce was amicable enough, in contrast to the spats that the girls were witness to throughout high school, which often involved flying objects and shattering glass that either Carla or Wendy would eventually clean up, not out of any sense of misplaced blame or guilt but because they didn't want to slice open their feet. Their mother kept the house in Thomasville as well as most of the family savings; their dad asked for only enough to get himself settled in Northridge.

Wendy could choose her mother but dismisses the idea. She's embroiled in the Thomasville Tennis Association and never home, anyway, spending every day that's remotely warm and sunny enough on the court, turning her body from its pale, soft shape that Wendy has long been used to into a sinewy, tan thing.

She drives straight to Carla's apartment. Although their fam-

70

ily home is big enough for both sisters to have moved back in, neither took the bait when their mother made the offer, and they're both smart enough to know that living together, though cheaper, would be a disaster. They're happy people now, happy in their professional lives and with each other, though Carla does have an annoying habit of constantly asking Wendy if she's seeing anyone.

Exhibit A: right on cue, when Carla pulls her apartment door open, she says, "Are you here to tell me something exciting?" Her eyebrows waggle obnoxiously.

"That depends on what you mean by exciting," Wendy says, shoving past her sister. People say they sometimes can't tell the two of them apart, which Wendy has never understood. She's at least four inches taller than Carla, and while yeah, maybe they have similar features, all of them are stretched a little wider in Wendy than in Carla: the broader bridge of her nose, the prominent brow, the eyes set further apart, the shoulders and back bigger but not in a beefy way, exactly. Wendy has the more pronounced hips and darker hair.

She sits down on Carla's couch. Her sister is also more austere in her decorative sensibilities: a few photos of the family on an end table next to a few candles that Wendy's never seen lit. One framed piece of art on the wall next to her television, a random dictionary page with a hand-drawn image of a green-eyed calico cat superimposed over the words. Wendy has never understood the appeal of this particular image because Carla doesn't own a cat. The family's never had a cat, or any other pets.

The apartment smells of lemon and herbs and some kind of meat, probably something simmering in Carla's old West Bend crockpot. Where Wendy is a good cook who enjoys fresh herbs and slicing fruits so their juices run over her fingers, Carla's idea of culinary activity is taking canned meats and pastas and throwing them in the slow cooker for five hours.

Wendy tosses herself on the couch and props her feet on Carla's coffee table, a rickety wooden thing she bought at Temera's Ephemeras when she moved home. Another difference between them: Carla still shops like she's a poor college student. McClain may not pay their administrative staff much, but they must pay her enough that she could stop buying her jeans secondhand at a consignment store.

Carla sits down on the other end of the sofa, stepping over Wendy's feet but not accosting her for the impropriety. Wendy's tempted to ask her if anything's been off at work, but then she remembers that nothing would seem strange to Carla; she has no way of knowing if anyone that she works with or for has disappeared.

"So, what's the news?" Carla's eyes are big, weirdly hopeful. She's always obsessed over Wendy's romantic life or, more properly, the lack thereof. Another way in which they are radically different: Carla can hardly go a week or two without having a boyfriend, or at least someone she's dating, a distinction that Wendy has never quite understood, at least in her sister's case, because for all her need to never be alone, Carla has not, as far as Wendy knows, gone out with more than one person at a time. Exclusivity is the name of her game.

But where Carla seems to find nourishment from companionship, Wendy does not. She tried in high school, identifying which boys she had crushes on when asked, but the truth was she really didn't have crushes on any of them; all she did was point and pick, and then the gaggle of girls she ate lunch with did the work of making magic happen. They had the uncanny ability to make any girl attractive to any boy, and Wendy found herself dragged to awkward movie dates and dinners at the Chinese buffet, nights that passed mostly in silence while she and her companion munched on fried crab rangoon and pretended to be humored by the fortunes in their cookies. There were rarely second dates, which didn't bother Wendy any because she hadn't really wanted the first dates. When she said as much to Carla during one of their phone calls, Carla was silent for a moment and then said, "Would you have rather dated girls?"

"I'd have rather dated no one."

"There's nothing noble about being alone."

"I never said there was."

She hadn't been sure then what she was trying to say or what she felt, because she had no words for it. The hormone-driven yearnings of her caveman-like male peers and the doting, giggly desires the girls that surrounded her were constantly chirping about felt foreign and wrong to Wendy, like there was some data input that she simply wasn't receiving, as if sexual and romantic desire was a tsunami whose waves were pounding everyone but her. It wasn't until college, when she was taking a course on feminist history for her junior interdisciplinary requirement that she was introduced to concepts such as aromanticism and asexuality. Hearing about them, something plunked deep in her gut with a satisfying splash, a knowledge that she'd found the right thing: that there were some people for whom sexual fulfillment meant no sex at all. That love, though present and possible, was largely, if not wholly, platonic. It didn't mean there was anything wrong with you; it just meant you were wired to want things in a different way.

Wendy has tried to explain this to her sister, but with middling results. It's as if using those words causes a form of acute disappearance, but instead of people, it's Carla's knowledge of the conversation that vanishes: something happens in her sister's brain whenever Wendy tries to explain that she's simply not interested in anyone that way. Wendy is

73

pretty sure that this isn't a matter of her sister being in denial: she really, truly cannot remember what Wendy tells her.

And so as soon as Carla is within reach, Wendy touches her sister's shoulder and says, "I think you should remember." Doug had said something like that to his roommate, and so had Merebeth to her wife. It didn't have to be anything special, as far as Wendy knew, and what is about to happen to her sister is weird enough—at least, Wendy assumes it will be—and she's never been one for great fanfare. And she hopes, desperately, that by making Carla remember that so many people from the real world are gone, she'll somehow manage to make Carla remember the things Wendy has tried to tell her over and over again.

CYNTHIA

SOMETIMES Cynthia wonders if she has vanished.

She knows this isn't true, and she also knows that to think this way is pride, one of the sins that mama scalded into her head when she was a child. Not everyone needs to be noticed, her mama might say. Awfully big of you to think you're that important. That you should be noticed.

But, also, her mama is gone, so who's to care what she has to say? This, too, is probably one of the seven deadly sins, but Cynthia isn't sure which. Wrath? But Cynthia's not angry about mama, not really, so she's pretty sure that isn't it.

Cynthia wears invisibility well, though. She's sure. Certainty isn't exactly pride, either, yeah?

A week after the disappearances, all anyone will talk about is who they've brought back to life.

That's the phrase half of them are using, *back to life*, as if anyone who doesn't know what's happened is dead. It bothers Cynthia for reasons she can't articulate, so she doesn't say anything. Instead, she does as she always does, which is keep her head down and do her work, trying to be humble but also fast—sloth looms, especially when no one is really paying attention to her—applying her heavy-duty hand lotion during lulls, stacking hot, clean platters on the wire shelves that terrified her at first, looking rickety and unstable and ready to fall over and crush her to death under a rain of thick porcelain. She only speaks when spoken to, smiling at Wendy's bad jokes and Merebeth's growling anger at the front of house boys, periodically spraying Doug with her hose when he gets to be too much.

No one has asked her about who she's chosen, even though just about everyone else has made someone in their life aware of the disappearances. Often enough Cynthia feels like a ghost, even though she knows she's being dramatic. Glenn's already given her two raises without her asking (she would never be so greedy as to presume she's deserving of anything beyond what she's been offered), and he's chummy with her in a way he's not to most of the staff, possibly because he knows—and he knows that Cynthia knows—that no one wants to wash dishes for a living, really, and she's good at it and doesn't seem to mind the work, which, aside from the way her hands go pruned and then bone dry, she doesn't.

She's glad enough for the anonymity, especially now. Doug has been hounding just about everyone, keeping track of their choices as if he's running some kind of laboratory experiment, going on and on about how he'd sorted out, now, that each of them can only give back one person's memory. This strikes Cynthia as sensible: if a bunch of people vanished and everyone was made to forget except a small handful of restaurant employees, and said employees could then start a chain reaction of remembering, what, then, was the point of the vanishings in the first place? Of course, she hasn't said so, because no one has asked her opinion, and in Cynthia's mind, sharing one's opinion without provocation or reason is a recipe for disaster. Plus, again: pride. Who cares what she thinks?

But she's also glad not to be asked because she wouldn't have an answer. While everyone else in the restaurant, it seems, has taken a quick route to deciding whom to revive—or awaken or remind or change or whatever; so many terms chosen and thrown around for it (careful, Cynthia, that we don't tip into wrath)—Cynthia hasn't felt the desire to make that choice. She knows Doug would go ballistic if he were to find out. Perhaps someone else, desperate for more than one person in their private life to remember, would pressure her to use her single shot on someone she hardly knows. At moments that feels like the best option, to give away the knowledge thrumming inside her to someone she'll never have to see again.

The problem is her family.

Daddy is in prison, at least as far as she knows. He went away when she was twelve, after he'd picked up not one or two DWIs but three, having lost his license and sapping the family's savings on his legal fees and failed attempts at rehab and AA, which Cynthia is now certain were simply smokescreens to keep him out of a prison sentence for blowing nearly a .3 his third time around. But then came his fourth run-in with the law, this one grisly and tragic: after a night at one of the local dives, Cynthia's daddy decided to drive down 63 toward Columbia, who knows why, she's never asked, and went the wrong way, causing a head-on collision with a van full of McClain students, killing three of them. They'd been on their way home from a spring break trip that they spent not gorging on tequila and cheap beer but working at a camp for people with disabilities, doing construction work through rain and unseasonable snow in South Carolina. Daddy was given a twenty-year sentence at the end of a trial that took six months, shipped off finally to Leavenworth to spend the next two decades by his lonesome. Mama, unable to manage the shame and guilt even though she'd done nothing wrong—she'd certainly not enabled his drinking, dumping any bottles she found hidden around the house down the drain and then arming herself with the empty glass if he threatened violence—moved away to rural Iowa to work as a seamstress in a dress shop, starting a new life for herself. Cynthia didn't leave, managing to get the job at Lake | Drive, which paid enough that she could afford a tiny studio apartment above the very bar that her daddy had been drinking at the night he killed those kids.

Mama had given birth to Cynthia when she was only seventeen, and when she left—when Cynthia herself was only seventeen but managed to pass herself off as old enough to sign a lease because the owner of the building had liked Daddy and was willing to pretend—she turned into a new woman; when Cynthia tried to call her for the first time, crying because she was feeling lost and dazed and discombobulated in an apartment all her own, her mama sighed into the phone and said, with great gentleness, "Sweetheart, I think I need a fresh start." It had taken Cynthia a long while to realize that this meant leaving her behind, not just physically but mentally, emotionally, severing ties with her only daughter for reasons that Cynthia would never understand. She found out later that her mama had found a new man in her tiny Iowa town who liked her stitchwork, had paid her to tailor his pants even though she had no idea what she was doing, and that lickety-split they were married and Mama was a mama again, this time to twins who could have been Cynthia's children, a boy named Cole and a girl named Connie. She thought of them as her younger siblings even though she'd never met them, seeing pictures only when Mama's friends with whom she was friends on Facebook commented on Mama's posts; Cynthia and Mama weren't friends, but Mama hadn't blocked her, either, so Cynthia felt connected to her, even if in secret.

She imagines driving up to Mama's house—Cynthia memorized the address the one time her mother gave her the information, before she had declared her intention to cut Cynthia out of her life—and laying her hands on her like they're in church, Cynthia offering a blessing. Although the deadly sins that have obsessed her since she was a child still thrum in her head, Cynthia stopped going to mass after her mother left her to herself. She'd never liked the motions and rituals, the incense that seemed to send its smoke flowing straight toward her, leaving her eyes watery. The priest at the only parish in Thomasville had a squeaky, angry voice, an octave too high to be particularly soothing but perfectly tuned for grating fire-and-brimstone. The first Sunday she skipped out on church she woke with her heart thumping fast; she was convinced that she would be struck down and tunneled straight away to hell. She wonders if Mama still prays or attends, dressing up little Cole and Connie in smart attire, a little clip-on tie for him and a warm, swishing dress for her, shushing them as they fidget in the uncomfortable pews, fingers trickling through the hymnal, eyes rolling as they pretend to follow along with the readings and Eucharistic Prayer. Maybe Mama has also abandoned her religiosity, another piece she felt the need to leave in the rearview mirror, shucked like everything else in her former life.

Doug is suddenly standing in front of her, staring from the other side of the dish pit, which Cynthia has always seen as part of a castle: sometimes it feels like a turret, the three slabs of industrial-strength steel that surround her the stonework from which she watches over everything else in the kitchen; other times it is a moat, sloughed with water and discarded kale and fries and gristle that she sprays away down the three drains; but then it also feels like a dungeon, the Hobart behind her with its grinding noise a medieval torture device, the racks for glasses the iron doors that shut her away from everything else.

"What?" Cynthia says by way of greeting, her voice soft, inquiring rather than braying. She's sure she's missed something he's said to her.

"The salad bowls," he says, pointing to the rack that's just come out of the dishwasher. "Can I have those?"

"Oh," she says. "Yes. They're still hot, though."

"That's okay."

Cynthia nods and squeezes herself against the station, the metal lip digging into her hip. She stares at the wall until she senses Doug is done grabbing up the bowls.

"Thanks," he says.

"Sure."

Cynthia watches him waddle back to the salad station. He's been asking everyone else about their choices, and yet nothing of her. A part of her grumbles and yearns, and she spends the next few minutes, as servers dump the detritus of sodas and beers into the bucket in the far corner of the dish station and scrape away potatoes and greens into the trash can she'll have to empty sooner than later, watching Doug do his work. His hands are nice, she realizes, his fingers long and tapered like a piano player's, careful as they grip vegetables and hanks of greens, delicately fluffing Romaine and iceberg lettuce in the salad bowls that he wipes down with a cool cloth first so that their heat doesn't wilt the vegetation. She watches him watching the servers as they come in and out through the swinging kitchen doors, most of their talk directed at one another or Merebeth or Wendy, sometimes Satiya if it's a question about dessert, today a lemon bar with raspberry jam sandwiched inside. Mostly, Doug's eyes follow Rion. His eyes rove over Rion's body, his gaze darting away when Rion looks anywhere near him. She blushes when she realizes that Doug, ostracized Doug, is in love.

She's watched how the servers cavort with one another; Doug has talked about it. Cynthia overheard him straight-up tell Rion that they all sleep together, but he left out what Cynthia has observed in their patterns of behavior: it's true that Timothie will hook up with anyone

80

who'll join him (he's flirted with her enough times, her face going red
when he winks and licks the edge of his lips), but she's seen how Carter
and Donny are really a pair, as is the case with Andre and Andrew. It's
true that none of them seem particularly monogamous—she's seen the
way they leave together in different combinations while she's pushing
the wheeled trash can out to the dumpster, how every now and then
Donny hops into Andre's car or Andrew leaves with Carter.

She watches these pairings with a fascination, equal parts achy and
off-put. For so long the threat of lust, that hot, angry demon she's been
taught to ward off, has loomed over her and her curiosities. Mama
never gave her the talk, and her teachers were always loathe to discuss
anything body-related; if a boy so much as whispered about an erection
or a girl even mentioned menstruation, her tight-lipped teachers went
rigid and were quick to condemn with threats of detention or suspen-
sion. For the majority of her young adulthood—and even now—Cynthia embraced the my-body-is-a-temple line of thinking, her virginity
a precious gift to be handed over only on her wedding night. Plenty
of times her body has hummed with yearning, her breath going shal-
low, her face blanching, her thighs achy. When she was thirteen, she
first reached down in the dark of night to the warm wet between her
legs, a want brought on by nothing. She spent a month feeling the
hard press of shame for giving in to that horrible deadly sin of wanton,
scattershot desire. Cynthia was plagued by nightmares of her demise
and damnation and managed to produce excuses for not taking com-
munion—which would have only exacerbated her sinful state until she
attended to confession and reconciliation—blaming the sudden onset
of her period, then feigning illness and other exhaustions, lightheaded-
ness that left her mama concerned that maybe she needed to be hauled
to the hospital. Eventually Cynthia's fear subsided, especially after she

81

snuck off one Saturday afternoon while Mama was napping, walking the mile to the church where she knew confession was on offer in the hour before five o'clock mass. She admitted, through the veiled wall that separated her from a faceless priest, that she had sullied herself by touching her body in unclean ways. She was told to recite three Hail Marys. Cynthia left feeling better, until the next time she felt the urge to touch herself.

When Rion is gone Doug returns to his salad preparation, squinting toward the tickets spewing out on his wheel. Dishes continue to stack up at the dish station. Cynthia flexes both of her hands, feels the cracks and dryness along her knuckles and fingertips. As she's loading a fresh rack of plates, a thought occurs to her: maybe she doesn't need to bring someone's memory back. As Rion comes clambering into the kitchen to collect an extra helping of balsamic from Doug, who freezes as he's about to pluck a trio of artichoke hearts out from their bin in favor of fulfilling Rion's request, Cynthia wonders if instead perhaps she can put a new thought, not a lost one, into someone's head.

PART THREE

YOU

YOU do not think you can be surprised. But to your surprise you are surprised.

They are smarter than you think.

Considering, caring, calculating. Consulting.

But you are proud, in a way. You do not show it, remaining tight-lipped, unimpressed, aloof from their jawing and discussing. The way they pry and wonder. They do not ask what you think, and so you hover around them, never inside their circle. But this does not bother you. You have always observed.

Your pride stems from their thinking and seeing. It gives you hope, the way they each muddle and meander, making decisions carefully—most of them, at least. They show a kindness that burrows deep, past the showy voices, the kind smiles and manufactured laughter all produced for the purposes of being paid, of earning one more dollar per table. What they do goes past niceness and into something more.

It fills you with a certain warmth; there's a beauty to it. And so you know that you've done the right thing.

DOUG

By the time Rion is approaching him at the squat rack Doug has already seen him. But Doug doesn't want to seem creepy, so he pretends not to notice until Rion is right there, tapping him on the shoulder. Doug turns, pulling his earbud from his right ear, and says, "Oh, hey."

Rion is wearing a sleeveless white cotton t-shirt, the sides home-cut so that half of his torso is visible on either side. He has lean, carved obliques, smooth skin, intercostal muscles that bite against the sides of ribs that Doug has to work not to stare at.

"I thought it was you," Rion says.

They're standing in the McClain rec center's weight room, early on a Sunday morning so the place is practically empty; two girls run on a pair of treadmills, and the sleepy attendant at the entrance keeps yawning and staring down at her phone, waiting for someone to ask for a spot or a towel to wipe down equipment. Every fifteen minutes she stands up and wanders around, armed with a gargantuan feather duster, making a lazy effort of wiping off machines that haven't been touched in an hour.

"It's me," is all Doug can think to say. Rion has shoulders that look like they've been chiseled from marble, drizzles of veins crowded at the front deltoids. Doug glances at himself in the mirror: he's sinewy, has his own little bumps of blood vessel at the surface of his skin, but he has had a hard time packing on much weight, probably because he jogs too much. He doesn't give his body enough rest and recovery or enough calories. It's as if surrounding himself with salads has nuked his ability to bulk up, even though he swallows down a trio of hard-boiled eggs every morning and suffers through chalky protein shakes before and after each shift at Lake | Drive.

"I don't think I've seen you here before," Rion says.

Doug looks around the room. One other guy, who is also here every morning bright and early, is grunting something fierce, his bald head the color of a ruby as he tries to hoist up a barbell laden with three forty-five pound weights plus a ten-spot on each end. The free weights section is totally empty, not a single bench in use.

"I come here in the morning," Doug says.

Rion nods and smiles. He's got huge dimples, and his blond-brown hair glimmers with summer. "I guess that's why. I'm usually not up this early."

"What's the occasion?"

Rion shrugs. "I woke up feeling fresh. Figured I might as well get my workout in before work. You on today?"

"Four o'clock," Doug says, sliding underneath the bar. He looks at Rion in the mirror. "As usual."

Rion waits, not offering a spot, while Doug finishes his reps. He makes extra sure to squat low and deep, pausing at the bottom. On the last one he falters, legs screaming displeasure two-thirds of the way up. Rion steps forward to help, but Doug finishes the move, clanging the bar into its place on the rack.

"Nice," Rion says.

"Thanks?" Doug says.

"I mean it. You have good form. Most people don't go low enough."

Doug looks at himself in the mirror. He's always been broad-shouldered—almost as much as Rion, he sees as they stand next to each other—but skinny, his collarbone and the nodes of his shoulders prominent pokes at the ends of his t-shirts. But his legs: years of riding his bike up and down his neighborhood streets, which snaked and dipped and rose like mountains, have given him a wider trunk at his hips, thighs that are hardly massive—he only squats one-eighty at the moment—but certainly bigger than his biceps and chest. He played soccer for a while in grade school and was relegated to the bench of the JV team in high school, but he kept at it, partly to be carried along on the wave of natural popularity that came with being on an athletic team, partly to see up close in the locker room the bodies of the boys he was jealous of, that he admired, and that he was in love with.

"Thanks," Doug says.

Rion is looking at him, not straight on but in the mirror. He tips his head to the side just-so, as if he's hearing someone or something for the first time. "Can I ask you something?"

"Okay," Doug says.

"You never hang out at the bar," Rion says.

"That's not really a question."

"I guess it isn't."

They look at one another in the mirror for a long moment. Doug preps for another set. He watches Rion watch him, and knows that his form is shit throughout. He pumps out an extra three reps to make up for it, his knees tingling, outer quads knotting when he releases the barbell.

"I guess I was wondering why you don't."

Doug shrugs. "Have to work, I guess."

"The bar stays open longer than the kitchen."

"Clean up takes a while."

"Evan never closes up until everyone's ready to leave."

Doug turns to face Rion straight on. The guy at the bench press is struggling again. The girl from the desk is wiping down the bench next to him, which, as far as Doug can tell, hasn't been used all morning. Her work leaves behind antiseptic streaks.

"Why do you care what I do or don't do?"

Rion looks hurt. "I was just wondering. You should hang out sometime."

"Oh," Doug says, feeling something deflate inside him while at the same time a weird, hard hope rises in his chest. He isn't sure what to say. Doug isn't like Scott, who demurs and dismisses talk of how good he is with guests during the lunch rush. He isn't like Rion, whom Doug has observed as being the kitchen ladies' favorite; they don't complain behind his back when he makes a special request or comes into their territory with a mistake needing correction, always kind and affable whether the screw up has been his fault or theirs. When Rion needs more dressing or a forgotten house salad on the fly, he's never commanding like Timothie, who Doug swears doesn't even see him. He's pretty sure his name has never come from Timothie's mouth. Which is why he tried to warn Rion, telling him about all the front of house boys and their carousel of carousing, hoping that this time someone would be different, that he might hold back, not be sucked into their musical chair game of who goes home with whom every night. And maybe he has been different; to Doug's knowledge, Rion hasn't sauntered out of the restaurant on the horny arm of one of his fellow servers.

"Well," Doug says, "thanks for the invitation."

"I mean it. It'd be nice to hang out."

Doug ignores the hard flush he feels creeping up his throat. Instead, he mumbles something about grabbing a drink of water. Rion

89

looks down, sees that Doug's bottle is right there at his feet. Doug slides past him and escapes across the weight room, past the girl at her desk. He drinks from the fountain, a long, thick glug, the water's cold biting against his teeth and gums. When he finally returns to the squat rack, Rion has moved on to one of the resistance towers where he's doing pullups. Doug sighs and watches the muscles in Rion's upper back twitch, sending out a message Doug desperately wishes he could read clearly.

◆

That night, a slow Sunday, the blitz of another Thomasville summer weekend having left everyone—staff, guests—sapped of energy by the time the sun begins to set, Rion is one of the first servers cut from the floor. Doug watches him finish up his side work: restocking the drinking glasses at the back station next to the ice machine, pouring out and scrubbing the tea urns except for the one he leaves behind for any late-night sippers that Timothie or Angela might wait on, detaching the nozzles from the soda machine and submerging them in a pitcher of water to dislodge gunk before wiping them clean. They haven't spoken all night, not until Rion has clocked out, apron wrapped up in a tight ball of pens and drinking straws. He stops at the salad station, where Doug, too, is about to finish up his night as soon as he cuts a batch of red onions for the morning.

"Hey," Rion says. Doug stops chopping, sets his knife down across his cutting board splattered with vegetal juices.

"Hi," Doug says.

"I'm having some people over tomorrow night. You should come."

"People?"

Rion shrugs. "Mostly the servers."

"The guys," Doug says.

Rion nods.

Doug's heart beats fast. He imagines red wine and low light and the sudden shedding of clothing, skin and muscles and lips moving over one another.

"To do what?"

"Mostly drink beer and bitch about work, probably. Maybe play some beer pong. You should come."

And then Rion is gone, out the kitchen, his laughter at something Timothie is doing at the drink station echoing in Doug's ears as he picks up his knife and goes back to his onions, begging silently that they don't make him weep.

◆

Rion lives in the Blue Apartments, a horseshoe-shaped cluster of two-story buildings, each divided into four units. They're high-demand, students setting up viewings and submitting rental applications a year before their leases will actually begin because they're right across the street from the McClain campus and despite this location they're inexpensive, a two-bedroom running only seven hundred dollars a month. They get their name from the buildings' sky-colored siding. Doug walks there on Monday evening at nine, leaving the house he shares with a roommate in the bowels of Thomasville's ramshackle residential neighborhood.

Rion lives on the second floor of a building on the horseshoe's left side. Between the buildings is a tiny lot where cars are parked at an awkward slant. He climbs the stairs to the second floor and knocks.

Almost immediately, the door opens: Rion stands before him in a green-and-yellow checked shirt, the sleeves rolled to his elbows. He's wearing thick-rimmed black glasses and looks a little bit like Clark Kent; the specs bring out his dimples. Rion smiles and says, "Glad you could make it," and gestures for Doug to enter.

The apartment is spacious, the living room home to two large brown couches with overstuffed cushions set at perpendicular angles to one another, both facing a large flat-screen television with a glass-topped table in between. Andre and Andrew are sitting on one couch, beer cans clenched in their fists, Carter and Donny on the other. Their drinks are on the table, their hands occupied by Nintendo 64 controllers. On the television screen, which is split in half, Mario and Luigi race on a dazzling rainbow-hued course.

"Something to drink?" Rion says, walking past the back of Andre and Andrew's couch toward a kitchen separated from the living room by a short countertop bar with two stools on the living room side. Before Doug can say a word, Rion opens the refrigerator and pulls out two cans of Natural Light, sliding one toward Doug while he opens the other and takes a long drink.

"I didn't think to bring anything," Doug says, picking up the can, which feels practically frozen. Little slakes of water dribble down the aluminum.

"I didn't ask you to. We have plenty."

"Okay," Doug says. "Do you live here alone?"

Rion lets out a bark of laughter. On the other side of the living room, past the front door, is a small hallway that, Doug will learn soon enough, leads to a bathroom and side-by-side bedrooms.

"My roommate went home for the summer. He still pays his rent."

Doug pops open his beer can and drinks. He's not sure what to say.

"Do you talk to him often?"

Rion smiles. "You want to know who I've made remember, don't you?"

Doug tries to match Rion's smile, but he feels sheepish heat flush up into his cheeks. He drinks again, the beer's coldness stabbing at his tongue so he can't taste anything. Doug doesn't go to many parties, and when he does he usually only manages to pilfer a beer or two here and there, mostly avoiding the junky shit the fraternities buy in large quantities. He doesn't quite hate the taste of beer; his tongue just hasn't gotten used to the sourness, the bitter yeast, the grassy muck.

"Come on," Rion says. "I'll give you the tour."

The tour is simply them moving back into the living room and then down the short hallway. Rion stops at the bathroom door. Inside, the vent fan whirs. "Donny did a number on it when he got here. I'd wait to piss if I were you." Then he points to the bedroom on the right, saying, "That's Eric's room. If you drink too much to get home, you can always crash there or on a couch."

"I walked."

Rion nods. "Smart."

He leads Doug into his bedroom, where Doug is assaulted by the smell of sandalwood. The room is dark except for a lamp sitting on a roll-top desk that is strewn with legal pads and textbooks. Rion's bed is a gigantic queen-size sleigh bed with dark navy-blue sheets and a matching comforter with white trim, the same design frilling the pillows arranged neatly at the top of the bed.

"Looks good," is all Doug can think to say. He's not sure what else he's supposed to say.

"So concludes the tour," Rion says, drinking from his beer. He swallows and crumples the can in his fist. "Another beer?"

93

"Oh." Doug looks down; he's barely drank from it and can see the metallic liquid swimming through the hole in the top. He takes a long drink and lets out a soft belch. "Sure."

In the living room, Andre has taken Carter's controller. Carter's head is lolling on the puffed-up back cushion, and he turns to look at Doug and Rion as they return. "Grab me a freshie?" he calls out, holding up his empty beer can. Rion nods and swerves toward the kitchen. Doug, not sure what to do, stands in the middle of the room, watching the cartoonish cars on the screen jostle and zoom and pummel one another with turtle shells and banana peels.

"You want winner?" Rion says, holding out a fresh beer can. Doug shakes his head.

"I've never played."

"That's okay. The learning curve is pretty simple. Small? Steep? What's the right word?"

"Gentle?" Carter offers, slapping his fingers together in a duckbill shape toward the beer Rion has not yet handed over.

Doug says, "I have no idea" and manages to finish his first beer before cracking open the second. His mouth tastes like coins smell.

"Well," Rion says, "there's no harm in losing. Come on. Sit."

It doesn't look like there's room on either couch for either of them, but Rion vaults over the back of Carter and Donny's sofa and wedges himself in between them. Andrew looks at Doug and pats the space between him and Andre, and Doug, thinking he really has no choice, steps around the far side of the sofa so he doesn't get in Andre's way and sits. Andrew and Andre's bodies loom large around him, even though neither is particularly gigantic. Like Rion, they're in decent shape, their t-shirts curling around their biceps like tightened cuffs, their midsections flat even as they sit curled forward. Andrew lets out a beery burp and wipes his lips with the back of his hand before taking a long glug from his drink, Adam's apple throbbing as he swallows. Doug tries, at first, not to let his knees knock against either of theirs, but such brushing is inevitable with them all crammed so close together. Neither Andrew nor Andre seem to notice the contact, so Doug tries to relax.

He takes the controller only one time, when Andre insists. Doug picks Yoshi, whom Rion says is a good choice. "Very agile. All-around solid." But Doug comes in ninth out of twelve cars, constantly skidding around corners and ramming into obstacles; twice he's squashed by a Thwomp and three times he slides right off the course and into the lava beneath, dragged out by a wormy-looking figure riding a cloud. Doug pretends to know who all of these characters are, silently nodding at references made by Donny or Andrew as cars go zooming around the course. In between races, the controllers are passed around—Rion apologizes more than once for only having two instead of four, but Doug just shrugs—and more beers are consumed, the empties collecting on the table like trophies. Eventually Carter says he's hungry, and suddenly everyone is lamenting the emptiness of their stomachs. Rion hops on his phone to order pizza. They keep playing, stopping only when a knock comes at the door. Andre shells out some cash for the tip, and the others are quick to grab their wallets and reimburse Rion before they gorge on the hot pizza, burning the roofs of their mouths on the steaming cheese and pepperoni.

When they're done eating, Donny lets out a belch and makes a throwing motion with his right hand, like he's tossing up a hook shot. "Pong time?"

"Pong time," Carter says.

Rion says to Doug, "You ever played beer pong?"

Doug shakes his head, feeling sheepish again, but Rion says, "That's okay. You can be my partner."

The first game is a mess. Doug and Rion play Andre and Andrew. Donny and Carter try to give Doug tips on form and strategy, but he feels like a lost cause. The ping pong ball is bulky and slippery in his hand, and he keeps throwing it either too far or too short or off to the side. Quickly, he and Rion are in a hole despite Rion's ability to land the ball in the cups with practically no splash. Andre is better than Andrew, so every time Andre misses Doug feels himself relax a little bit because they won't get the balls back (if nothing else, Doug figures out the rules of the game fast).

The one thing he is, however, is quick with his hands thanks to all of that chopping and slicing and plating. When one of his shots banks off the front-most cup, he grabs the ball up when it rolls back past the halfway mark of the table, which grants him the opportunity to take a dubious behind-the-back shot, which requires him to curl his right arm behind his body as he tries to sink it in a cup. By some miracle, when he lets the ball fly, it lands in a cup. Not one of four that he and Rion need to make still in order to win the game, but one sitting in front of Andrew, who has not finished drinking yet.

"Death cup!" Donny yells.

"Holy shit," Carter says, beaming.

Doug looks at Rion. "What's death cup?"

Rion is busy laughing, his face cherry. He slaps the table and offers Doug a high-five, who accepts but frowns. Andre is shaking his head while Andrew stares down at his cup, the ping pong ball bouncing in the beer.

Donny explains. "Death cup is where if someone makes a cup you haven't finished drinking yet, you lose." He looks down at the table, where Andrew and Andre had only one cup left to make. "No matter the score."

Doug looks at Rion. "So, we won?"

Rion smiles. "We sure did."

◆

Though they're all wasted at one in the morning, Andre and Andrew and Donny and Carter say their goodbyes and stumble out into
the night, reassuring Rion that they're walking. Doug, watching, understands implicitly that they'll be going home in pairs. When he imagines what they'll be doing after they arrive at their destinations, he feels
flush.

He's proud of himself for not puking, though after the third game
of beer pong, after he finally figured out how to shoot so that he at least
made a cup every now and then, he felt a wave of nausea come over
him, though that could have been from Rion clapping him on the back
every time Doug did something remotely useful, even if it was simply
to swat a ball away when someone—usually Donny—tried to sneak
in a bounce for a double-cup takeaway. Rion's hand was warm; Doug
could feel the heat through his t-shirt. Rion had strong fingers, cal-
louses from lifting weights, tapered nails.

When they're the only two in the apartment, Doug isn't sure what
to do. Rion, after closing the door behind Carter, throws himself over
the back of one of the couches, surprisingly agile for being so bombed,
and lays out across the cushions.

"One more round of MK?"

"Sure," Doug says, blood pounding in his face. Because Rion is
splayed out over the entirety of his couch, Doug sits on the empty one.

Rion sits up, grunting and flailing but ultimately righting himself.

97

As he plucks one of the controllers from the table, he says, "I'm glad you came tonight."

"Me too," Doug says.

"And you haven't said a word about the disappearances."

Doug's face feels warm. "Sorry."

Rion smiles. "I'm just giving you a hard time. I'm surprised more people don't have more to say. It's super weird."

"It is."

"You have any new theories?"

"Theories?" Doug says. His heart is beating fast in his chest. Rion punches buttons on the controller and they each choose their characters. Doug goes for the princess for no good reason.

"Like, why we can remember, why no one else can, why we can make someone remember, but only one someone." He laughs at himself. "'One someone.' God, I'm definitely drunk." He smiles and looks at Doug. "Sorry."

"It's okay," Doug says. They start their first race, and Doug is quickly mired near the back of the pack.

"I think it's good that you're invested. It doesn't seem like most people care much that so many people are gone."

Doug nods, his princess crashing out on a banana peel, her car spinning in an angry circle. He feels a prickliness on the back of his neck. If anyone else at Lake | Drive cares about the vanishings, they bury that concern, as if it's uncouth or uncool to express worry. How no one feels themselves unraveling constantly since people simply blinkered out of existence and were replaced by a bunch of strangers Doug can't begin to understand. Even now, here, drunk and warm and sleepy and starting to think that maybe something will happen between him and Rion, as his video game princess comes tumbling across the finish line in seventh, which isn't too bad, he feels a roil in his gut at knowing that the world is off-kilter. He hasn't gone a day without wondering what has happened to those who are gone: how can lives, memories, all traces be erased just like that? Doug tries to imagine his entire being, every piece of himself he's left behind in the world for the last twenty years, simply snapping out of existence. Everything gone. It makes him dizzy.

They complete their second race in silence. Rion wins easily, and this time Doug comes in fourth, though neither says anything about his improved performance. The only lights on in the apartment are in the kitchen and the bathroom, where one of the other Lake | Drive boys has left the vent fan whirring.

"Tell me about you," Rion says when they're midway through the third race.

"What?"

"Tell me something I don't know about you."

"Why?"

"Because I want to know more about you."

"Why?"

Rion rolls his eyes but concentrates on the race. Doug has managed to pull into the lead, briefly, though he's bombed by a blue shell and one of the computer characters passes him.

"Unlucky," Rion says.

"Story of my life," Doug says.

When they've finished their last race, Rion yawns and leans his head back on the couch, eyes rolling toward the ceiling, where Doug sees nothing of interest. Rion seems to have forgotten about his inquiry about Doug, who sets his controller down.

"I should probably head home," he says.

"Getting late," Rion says, but Doug can't tell whether this is his way of agreeing, of booting Doug out, or suggesting he stay the night. When Doug stands, so does Rion, who slaps his thighs and lets out a yawn, followed by a hard belch. They move around in an awkward dance toward the door, Rion saying again how grateful he is that Doug came, Doug thanking him for the invitation, Doug opening the apartment door, Rion looking out into the dark, Doug following his gaze, Rion saying nothing, Doug stepping outside, Doug saying, "Good night, then," Rion nodding, Doug walking down the wooden steps, the building rattling, Rion watching, Doug looking back, the darkness swallowing him as he hits the concrete of the parking lot, the sound of the door closing rattling in his head, the heat, that summer heat, glazing him with want and regret.

◆

Doug doesn't see Rion the next morning at the weight room, where he sweats out his hangover with bench presses and a core circuit that leaves his abs and shoulders burning. His shift at Lake | Drive feels endless—Rion isn't there, either—and is comprised mostly of making dinner salads and listening to Donny bitch about how dehydrated he is.

He's tired and ready for bed when he finally clocks out, waved away just before nine by Merebeth, but when he walks out of the restaurant, he stops halfway through the parking lot because Rion is sitting on the hood of his car.

"Hey," Rion says.

"Hi." Doug can feel the night's squeezing warmth, the dampness of the air a heavy blanket pressing down on his shoulders.

"How are we feeling today?"

"I think my hangover's finally dissipating," Doug says.

"Heck of a Monday night, that's for sure," Rion says. He's wearing white board shorts and a blue t-shirt and looks like he belongs on the California coast. A night breeze lifts his hair. His feet are perched on the tiny lip of rear bumper. Rion looks totally relaxed compared to how Doug feels, which is like the ground might open up at any moment and swallow him. He feels a thrill, but a part of him, the part sending his heart into a sprint and making his fingers shake, wishes he could be one of the vanished.

"What are you doing here?" Doug says. "On your day off, I mean."

Rion smiles and hops down from the car, which rocks as he dives off. He holds out a set of keys. "I had an idea."

"An idea?"

"An adventure."

"An adventure?" Doug feels like an idiot, able only to parrot what Rion is saying.

"If you're up for it."

Doug says, "Sure." Of course he is, even if he's exhausted. He can feel the puffiness around his eyes, the droop of his shoulders. His feet feel like lead.

Rion rattles the keys. "I checked with Perry that no one is booked for The Drive tonight. And Satiya let me borrow the keys."

"The keys?"

"To the golf cart."

"Oh."

Rion spins them around on his index finger. "I thought we could check it out. Have you been there?"

Doug shakes his head.

"Come on, then."

They walk around the side of the building, past the stink of the dumpster and grease disposal to the small garage attached to the back of the private dining room. Someone has left the door open for them, so they climb directly into the golf cart, which feels plush and luxurious, but that could be a matter of Doug's exhaustion. He and Rion sit side by side, Doug's left thigh brushing Rion's right. As he turns on the ignition, Rion smiles at him. And then they're off.

Rion drives the cart carefully, staying in the center of the asphalt path. The lake smells briny, as though they're on the edge of an ocean. Doug closes his eyes and imagines he's being whisked away to some exotic locale, the Bahamas or Aruba or, hell, even someplace like Long Beach or Santa Monica. He's never left Missouri except for one trip to Chicago to visit cousins that he hasn't seen since he was sixteen years old. Doug's parents are homebodies, his father managing a feed outlet in Macon, his mother teaching math at the local grade school. When Doug decided to go to McClain, they were tight-lipped if proud, and they have only ever made the hour drive to see him twice: first when helping him move into his dorm, and second for parents' weekend his sophomore year, which they spent clutching their hands together as Doug led them through the quad and the library and academic buildings and then took them to window shop on the square. His parents went wide-eyed at all of the bars, which were surprisingly packed on an early Saturday afternoon, the McClain students apparently funneling their fancy for college football into Mizzou's team, as their own division two squad was nothing to write home about.

Doug opens his eyes when Rion brings the golf cart to a halt in front of the gazebo closest to the water.

"Nice dream?" Rion says.

Doug blushes. "I wasn't actually asleep."

"It's possible to dream while awake, don't you think?"

"I guess."

"So, where'd you go?"

Doug isn't sure what to say, but Rion doesn't press, hopping out of the cart and looking toward the water, which is glazed with the shimmer of stars. The sky is open and clear and constellations Doug doesn't know wink in bright splatters. He follows Rion into the gazebo, where the single table for four is bare. Doug feels the briefest ache of disappointment; he'd half-expected some grand gesture on Rion's part, that the fairy lights strung about the gazebo's roof would be ablaze, along with dozens of candles, romantic music and wine, maybe even Timothie, smirk and all, serving as sommelier and waiter. But everything is dark minus the moon and starlight, the only sounds the honk of bullfrogs and bugs.

"It's nice out here," Rion says, wandering in a slow circle, looking up at the pitched interior of the gazebo's roof as if it's covered in a Da Vinci masterpiece. When Doug looks up, all he sees is unvarnished wood and exposed carpenter's screws. He glances at Rion, who looks like a kid in a museum, full of wonder.

"It is nice," Doug says.

Rion stops walking, standing behind one of the table's chairs, on which he rests his hands. He inhales and says, "I don't think I've ever had a reason to bring someone somewhere like this."

Doug is standing on the other side of the table, hands placed on the back of the chair in the exact same manner as Rion's. "What do you mean?"

Rion shrugs. "I've never had someone I've wanted to make such a gesture to. Glamming up out here, having someone cook for you there." He points a thumb over his shoulder toward the second gazebo, where the stainless steel appliances wink in the night. "It would take something—someone—special."

Doug nods, feels a wave of boldness, and says, "But here we are."

Rion nods and smiles. "Yes. Here we are."

◆

The next night, they finish work at the same time. Instead of hovering at the bar for his usual nightcap, Rion asks if Doug wants to go to the lake.

"But we could walk this time."

Doug's heart beats in his throat as they leave the restaurant, no sneaking this time. He tries to ignore the clucking noises Donny makes and the low whistle that comes from Carter. Evan smiles as they walk toward the bump-out, which has a door leading onto a small promenade with a set of steps leading down to the path that heads toward The Drive. The bannisters are covered in tubed lights, plastic protecting them from the elements. They're lit, and their illumination traces warm shadows over Rion's features, under-lighting his jawline and cheekbones. Doug tries not to stare, but he's starting to think that Rion wouldn't mind.

They walk the quarter-mile in silence. Rion seems comfortable with the quiet, not stumbling or stretching to fill it with noise, so Doug relaxes into the sounds of the late evening. The breeze rustles the scutch grass and chops the water, dizzying the surface with dancing silver. The frogs croak, the katydids hum. These are noises that Doug grew up with, and their summer song relaxes him, easing the churn in his stomach. He still isn't sure what Rion wants; they sat on the gazebo for a long time last night, telling one another their life stories. Doug talked about his parents and their strange fears of the outside world, which elicited a half-smile from Rion. Doug was quick, in his telling, to separate himself from his parents' outlook, for which he later felt a weird shame, not because it was untrue—Doug desperately wanted, and still wants, to see more of the world—but because he felt bad speaking about them in such a negative way. Rion told him about his own family, large, five kids, Rion squashed right in the middle, with two older brothers both already out of college and two younger sisters still in high school. When he was a kid—nine or ten—he had dreams of being an actor. Mostly for the money, he supposes now, and the fame, because he didn't really have any idea what it meant to take on a role.

"It was easy to get lost in the shuffle," Rion said, his voice going low for the first time. Doug could hear the sorrow in it. "I think being on the stage made me feel remembered."

Doug was tempted for a quick moment to ask if Rion would choose any of his siblings to give their memory back, but he held his tongue: Rion hadn't brought up the disappearances, and Doug didn't want to seem any more obsessive than he already did. And he was obsessed, of course. The restaurant staff were, as far as he could tell, the only people in the world who had any idea that anything had changed, and yet most of them simply went through their days earning tips and searing filets like nothing had gone wrong or shifted out of balance.

They reach the gazebos, but Rion keeps walking, off the asphalt and into the grass, which has been recently mown. By whom, Doug has no idea. Maybe Glenn, trying to halt his tailspin, has gone on a transcendentalist jag, throwing himself into landscaping work. But Doug can't imagine Glenn on a lawn mower or doing any real work besides propping up a barstool.

"You ever been in it?" Rion says.

"In what?"

Rion gestures at the water.

"The lake?"

"Yeah."

"No."

Rion flashes him a grin, his smile wolfish in the moonlight. "Well, first time for everything."

"You want to go in the lake?"

"Why not?"

And then, before Doug can say anything else, Rion is removing his clothes. First comes off his shirt, the white button down peeled away to reveal a ribbed undershirt that he pulls over his head with sinuous grace. Doug tries not to stare at Rion's torso, muscled and craggy and immediately bringing heat to Doug's cheeks. Then, without hesitation, Ryan is pulling off his shoes. His belt tinkles as he unbuckles it. As if he's alone, in his bedroom, Rion slips his pants off, steps out of them, and kicks them back onto the asphalt. Then, in a smooth swipe that leaves Doug's mouth full of saliva, Rion peels down his underwear. Even in the shadowy dark, the pale of his backside shines. Rion is facing away from Doug, but he turns, the muscles of his back and neck twisting.

"Well?" Rion says. "Come on."

Doug shakes as he pulls off his shirt, the night's warmth caressing his bare stomach, which he tries to suck in. He fumbles with his pants, even though they're kitchen utilities and don't have a belt. He pulls them down, and then pauses in his underwear. The grass tickles at his toes. Rion is already moving toward the water, pushing through the high stalks at the bank that whoever mowed didn't bother with. While Doug stands in his boxer shorts, Rion leaps right in, body disappearing into the water with a splash. A second later he breaks the surface. Rion shakes his head, sending a spray of water around; Doug is sure a few sprinkle at his calves, but that could all be in his head.

"Coming in?" Rion asks, arms like eels slithering just under the surface.

Doug, under Rion's hot gaze, pulls off his underwear and tries to ignore the magma-like heat in his cheeks. Then, before he can change his mind, he leaps in. The water is like bathwater, lukewarm and thick with silt when he lets some in his mouth.

"It's deeper than I thought," Rion says when Doug surfaces. "But it feels okay."

Doug nods. He's not sure what to do, what comes next. They bob in the water, faces slick, shoulders buoying up and down. Rion is smiling. His hair is flattened down across his forehead and water drips down his face like he's in an advertisement for cologne or underwear. Doug is acutely aware that they're both naked, and he resists the urge to glance down into the mirror-reflective water to try to glimpse Rion's lower body.

"Ever done this before?" Rion says.

Doug lets out a small laugh and shakes his head, which makes Rion smile more brightly.

"Me neither."

"Not sure I believe you."

"Why not?"

"You seem comfortable."

Rion tips his head back and looks up at the stars. His chest and stomach tilt out of the water, the flare of his hipbones wrapped in lean muscle teasing at the surface. Rion's groin is still narrowly under the water; in the dark, the shape of his genitals is murky and ill-defined. A tiny crop of pubic hair peeks out.

"I guess it's the company," Rion says. He dips his head beneath the surface and Doug frowns, watching the pale slip of him. When Rion emerges, he bobs right in front of Doug. Water drips off his lips, which are plump and pursed.

And then, before Doug can say a word, Rion kisses him. The kiss is not long, barely a brush; their lips are too wet for purchase, tongues tinged with the muck of lake water.

"You taste like cherries," Doug whispers.

Rion laughs and then kisses him a second time. He pulls Doug close, their hips brushing under the surface, a touch that feels like ignition. Rion slides one hand around Doug's back, the other cradling his chin. Doug parts his lips and lets Rion's tongue in, and then he is holding Rion, too, his hands pressed against Rion's back, where he can feel the muscles sliding around his spine like a protective phalanx. A part of him feels embarrassed that he's got an erection, that it's poking obnoxiously at Rion's thigh, but the rest of him doesn't care. He lets Rion kiss him, lets their warm, wet bodies collide, knees knocking under the water, toes jamming together as they both tread, neither concerned that the other will sink.

◆

Doug jerks awake. For a moment he's crushed by a hard press of disappointment, convinced that it was all a dream. It has happened before, that he's been wrenched from pleasant sleep by his alarm clock, pulled from a glorious nightscape filled not necessarily with sex but romantic intimacy, his body lolled against another, Doug's head in someone's lap as their hands wend their way through his hair. Every time he's greeted by his otherwise empty bed, the stark walls of his bedroom, the

108

noise of his roommate Nolan flushing the toilet.

But then he smells the lake on his skin. His lips are chapped and dried out, but they retain Rion's taste. Doug's back tingles at the memory of his touch, as if Rion's hands have scorched their imprint onto his skin.

Early morning light is searching for space between his blinds. Doug rolls over and checks his phone: nearly six. He and Rion stayed at the lake, laughing and splashing each other after the kissing was over, until nearly midnight. They raced to the center and treaded water there, kissing again, Rion nibbling at Doug's shoulder, his hand grazing Doug's thigh. Every touch was a new light, a shuddering pleasure. When they returned to land, they laid on the warm asphalt until they were dry, and then they put on their clothes and walked back to the restaurant. The parking lot was practically empty, Evan and Merebeth's the only vehicles in the lot.

Doug takes a deep breath and holds it in his chest until his lungs ache and his eyes start to water. He lets it out slowly. When he breathes again, his ribs throb with thanks. He tries to fall back to sleep, but he can't help remembering how Rion split away as they walked toward their cars, parked with only one empty space between them. When Doug looked toward him, Rion shook his head and said, as if reading his mind, "It's better to do things the right way."

He thought about that on his drive home, during which he felt drunk. Doug's desire for Rion throbbed at the back of his head. Halfway home, his phone chirped: a text from Rion saying *Thanks for a good night*. Doug spent the rest of his drive, headlights blipping across trees and out-of-control grass and the first vestiges of Thomasville proper, trying to figure out what to say back. He waited until he was parked, and then, with trembling fingers, he wrote: *I had a great time*. Rion's response came fast: *See you tomorrow.*

Doug's body feels tingly with both want and satisfaction. The truth is, he's glad things didn't progress further. He watches the boys of Lake | Drive tumbling away with one another and feels endless jolts of bewildered jealousy at the ease with which they hook up. Doug's only real sexual experience came in high school when he was a senior. A girl from the theatre club who sat in front of him in pre-calculus turned around one afternoon and said, "Come to the play this weekend, will you?" She slapped a ticket onto his desk. The theatre program at his dinky public high school was hardly robust, and in an effort to increase audience size, every member of the spring play had been tasked with distributing five tickets, none to family members, and the girl, Lauren, was playing the lead in a production of something Doug had never heard of. He wouldn't remember the plot or anything about the play because, after the final curtain call by the cast, Lauren appeared outside, rushing up to him as he walked to his car in the half-empty parking lot. She grabbed him around the bicep and thanked him for coming. He was, she said, the only one of her five ticket recipients who'd done so. Something sparkled in her eyes, which lasered in on her grip around his arm, as if she was surprised that there was anything muscled there at all. She looked Doug over, and, tilting her head, said, "You wanna hang out?" An hour and a half later, after they'd sucked down milkshakes at the one decent ice cream place in town, he was in her empty house— parents out of town, despite her big acting debut—and suddenly in her bedroom, on her bed, his clothes coming off, body thrumming with confused, adolescent want.

Doug thought the loss of his virginity would open a gateway, opportunities appearing in waves as soon as he had that first experience tucked away. But even Lauren started ignoring him the very next week, as if their encounter had never happened; she moved to a different seat in pre-calc, as though he was a pariah. He had no idea if he'd performed poorly—he wasn't stupid, so he was pretty sure the answer was yes, but wasn't that the case for everyone's first time?—but he didn't think that demanded a sudden casting-off. He finished high school telling no one about this sexual check-mark. Then as college began, he found himself too bruised by Lauren's rejection to seal the deal on the few occasions that Doug thought he was in a position to do so.

With guys, the prospects were worse. Doug had long known he was bisexual, his adolescent attractions flying far and wide. This was a secret he kept to himself; middle Missouri, after all, dusty and small and conservative, was hardly a place to be out and proud. His high school didn't have a gay-straight alliance. No one talked about gender identity, and rainbow flags were nowhere to be found in the school's halls or on any neighborhood doors or yards. Doug long thought about telling his parents the truth if for no other reason than to ease the heaviness in his chest at carrying part of who he was inside with no release, but he had no idea how they might react. On the one hand, he could see them being kind and encouraging, gathering him up in hugs; on the other, he could see their eyes shifting uncomfortably, scanning him for evidence of his strangeness, his deviance (a word he could hear coming from his dad's twangy lips); on yet another, he could picture them stiffening, scowling, and booting him from their lives forever. And while Doug liked to imagine he could be brave and independent and self-sufficient, he was only eighteen and knew nothing about the world beyond the narrow borders of his small life. So, he sewed himself up, kept quiet, ached and wandered through his final months of high school until he could escape, even if said escape was north, further into the rural land-scape of the Missouri-Iowa border zone, to Thomasville and McClain

State.

It didn't feel like much of an escape. Yes, Doug finally found his rainbow flags and his genders and sexualities clubs and outspoken young people talking about being queer and transgender and asexual. He found professors with pink triangles on their office doors and coursework where the literature featured gay sex scenes that didn't shy away from detail. But still, he found himself unable to pierce his way into that queer world. How to know who would be interested and who wouldn't? While there were certainly some signs—one of the bars held an LGBT night once a month, all the out kids flocking to the downtown square whether they were old enough to drink trashy beer and cheap vodka or not—and it was, after all, the twenty-first century, and there were apps for finding people willing to hook up with. But Doug, despite the desert island that was his sex life, was a romantic, waiting for what he thought of as the real thing, the kind of love story that you saw on television and the big screen, a chance encounter with a soul mate dropping you into a charming storyline and a happily-ever-after.

Ridiculous, of course. He told himself this all the time.

But now.

He lays in bed for a long time, floating in and out of light sleep until the sunshine pushing through the blinds becomes too much. Doug sits up, gathers his phone—no new messages from Rion—and wanders out into the living room, where Nolan is perched on the couch, watching ESPN. He's an over-caffeinated chemistry major who loves anything sports-related; he even owns an old, boxed version of *Jeopardy!* full of ephemeral sporting trivia, the answers to which he can recite like he's in the middle of a lightning round of a trivia competition. He's always frazzled-looking, with spazzy hair and rosy cheeks and tremulous hands, his knees bouncy the moment he sits down anywhere.

"I still can't believe it." Nolan gestures toward the television. "Like who the hell is this world number one in tennis that's in the quarterfinals at Wimbledon?"

That's how Nolan has spent the week since Doug brought his memory back: staring at the television, scrolling through Twitter, searching various sports websites, trying to reckon with the disappearances of those whose careers he has spent his young adulthood following.

"Eggs?" Nolan says, pointing down at the smeary plate sitting in front of him.

"I'm good," Doug says.

Nolan grins. "You were late coming home last night."

Doug says nothing. He and Nolan met when they were in the same freshman composition class, paired together for their final research project; their teaching assistant instructor was lazy in that way, finding ways to reduce his grading load at any opportunity. Doug was the better writer, but Nolan enjoyed research, perusing the library database from which they were required to pull at least six academic articles. He overdid it, printing off a dozen for them to use. Doug fashioned decent-enough sentences and paragraphs, integrating their quotes with what their instructor called "solid framing and good contextualizing." They received an A, and they became friends, finding a ramshackle rental house a few blocks from campus when their compulsory freshman year in the dorms was over. Doug has never come out to Nolan overtly, and he's sometimes wondered about his roommate's own predilections; Nolan doesn't seem to ever find himself in emotional entanglements, either, neither of them making any habits of bringing strangers home at night. Their bedrooms share a wall, and the walls aren't particularly thick, so if either one was getting their jollies off, the other would likely know about it.

"I was at work," Doug says, tossing himself down on the couch. They bought most of their furniture from Temera's Ephemeras, the rest left behind by the house's previous renters, a pair of senior sorority girls who, the day Nolan and Doug toured the property, gave Nolan and Doug their phone numbers and eventually texted them, asking if they wanted the recliner and couch, a pair of muddy-brown things that have been part of the house, apparently, for nearly a decade. Doug and Nolan could think of no reason not to keep the tradition going.

Nolan grins and scoops the last of the egg from his plate and says, "Uh huh. Busy night?" He worked at a restaurant in high school as a busboy before he left for college; Doug knows he knows that a weeknight, in Thomasville, in summer, wouldn't demand that he be stuck at Lake | Drive until nearly midnight.

"Something like that," Doug says.

"Look at this," Nolan says. "They're talking about the best NBA players of all time and LeBron is nowhere to be found." He shakes his head. "This is all really tragic."

After Doug accidentally fixed Nolan's memory, Nolan offered to try to bring someone else's back on Doug's behalf. But Doug shook his head, even when Nolan suggested one of Doug's parents as the beneficiary. He couldn't imagine how it would really change his parents' life if they remembered how things were supposed to be. Doug had checked that both of them were still around, making an innocuous phone call to check in, as he did every few weeks, a ritual that had begun when he was a shy, scared freshman who had no one else to talk to. His mother had answered the phone, and, as was their routine, his father picked up the second landline in their bedroom—Doug knew no one else who still had a landline, much less a second receiver—and he felt a wash of relief that neither of them had vanished. After they'd hung up, his mother telling him about the newest round of budget cuts coming to the school and the increase in her class size ("We don't have any space for more desks, so I have no idea what we're going to do. Can you believe it?") and his father starting in on something about one of his part-time employees stealing landscaping gravel from the supply store, Doug had felt a weird numbness: if one of his parents had been erased, what would he have felt? He realized, with a guilty shock, that he might have felt very little. Even, possibly, a bit of happiness, if one of his parents was replaced by someone more exciting, someone who didn't want to do the same thing every day, living the same mediocre life in sleepy rural Missouri until it was time to retire. So at Nolan's offer, Doug quietly rejected the idea while also suspecting it didn't work like that. He had no real reason to think this way; there was no evidence that Nolan wouldn't be able to give someone else their memory back, at least not until the next day when, after Nolan spent a night out at the bars, he told Doug he'd tried it and it hadn't worked.

"Unless I did it wrong," he'd said.

Doug had shrugged. What could right and wrong mean in a situation like this? What rules could there possibly be?

Nolan stands and takes his plate to the kitchen. Doug watches the television, listens to the sound of Nolan scrubbing the dishes. They're both good about cleaning as they go about their business, never letting dirty plates and cups pile up in their sink, quick to take out the trash when it starts to mound in the can next to the countertop. They take turns vacuuming the shag carpet each Sunday afternoon, scrubbing the bathroom floor and spraying down the shower, digging goop off of the mirror and out of the clamshell sink. Doug's appreciative of this attention to cleanliness.

What he's not a fan of, sometimes, is Nolan's observational prowess, which he demonstrates when he plops back down on the sofa, plucks up the remote, and mutes the tv. He crosses his arms and stares at Doug.

"So, spill."

"Spill what?"

"Don't play stupid, Douglas. You're not good at it."

"I don't—I don't know."

Nolan leans forward. "Just tell me what happened." There's light in Nolan's voice, not mockery but excitement, a desire to hear something good. So, Doug takes a deep breath and tells him.

◆

The afternoon is a long, slow march toward his work shift. Usually the days go by too fast, four o'clock zooming up before Doug feels like he's had time to accomplish anything. He goes to the gym, later than usual so there are more people than he likes; he has to reorganize the order of his workout when all of the benches are in use. Doug hopes to see Rion, but he doesn't appear. Maybe he came in the morning, hoping to see Doug. Doug runs on the treadmill for a while when he's finished lifting weights. He pushes the speed and incline to more than he's used to, and he's breathing hard fast. Sweat blooms across his t-shirt, seeping from his armpits and lower back and at his sternum. Doug walks home through the afternoon heat, his body throbbing, quads tight and chest soaked with lactic acid, the humidity and sunlight sending him into a second sweat, so drenching that he struggles to pull off his t-shirt when he wrings it out on the front porch, leaving a wet puddle on the wood. It has already evaporated when he leaves for work, his body still belabored by tiredness.

Pulling into the Lake | Drive parking lot, Doug is hit with a sudden nerviness: he wonders who will know what. Rumor and gossip pass fast through restaurants like contagion; as soon as one of the servers has hooked up with another, everyone seems to be aware. But Doug and Rion didn't exactly hook up. On the other hand, they didn't exactly not. Doug wonders how Timothie and Carter and Donny and all will look at him: will he be one of them now, pulled into their weird sexual fold, even though he's still back of the house? Will Merebeth and Wendy smirk in his direction? Will Cynthia spray him more or less with the hose?

Rion isn't there.

"Called out sick," Merebeth says when Doug manages to ask with as much inconspicuousness as he can muster. Doug nods, wondering if Rion will still have a job, a question that makes him queasy. Glenn has a pretty harsh no-show-no-job policy, but Merebeth, as if she can read his mind, assuages him quickly, saying that Scott agreed to stick around for the night shift, emerging from behind the bar to take up Rion's section when Rion called to see if anyone was available to cover for him.

The night sloughs by slowly. The floor is weirdly dead. The bump-out isn't open, and there's no reservation for The Drive. Doug has plenty of time to sneak glances at his phone. He sends a text to Rion, wishing him a speedy recovery and hoping he feels better soon; his fingers tremble as he types, and he glances around the kitchen to see if anyone notices, but Cynthia is staring at the Hobart as if it's a crystal ball and Merebeth is using the dead hours to work on inventory, counting steaks in the cooler drawer while Wendy preps a plate of frites, waiting for the petit sirloin on the grill to finish cooking. No one notices anything he's doing. The servers, too, seem to know nothing at all. Doug feels like a ghost, and he's not sure if he's happy or sad about it.

Rion doesn't respond to his message, which Doug tells himself means that he's laid up in his bed or on his couch, body covered by a pile of blankets despite the summer swelter. Doug thinks he should make some kind of gesture, show up with chicken soup or cold medicine or something, and during the last hour of his shift—Glenn appears, sighing at the emptiness of the restaurant, and tells Doug to restock his station and get out of there—his imagination runs wild with ideas, but when faced with the reality of doing something, his built-up plans come crashing down, his chest feeling strangled at the idea of showing up uninvited. He can picture Rion frowning, perplexed and annoyed that his recovery sleep has been interrupted. Doug pictures Rion taking the soup or whatever and dismissing Doug with a tight smile, door not quite slammed but not shut with gratitude either. When he clocks out, Doug doesn't bother looking in on the dining room to see if any of the server boys are sitting down for cocktails and instead slips out into the night without saying goodbye to anyone.

The weekend trudges by in similar fashion, Rion gone for the entire Friday, Saturday, Sunday march. Doug feels off-kilter all weekend, and it seeps into his work; he misses substitution requests on a niçoise and several wilted salads, and he places the wrong dressings on so many dishes on Saturday night that Glenn yells at him, leaving everyone blinking in surprise. Glenn raises his voice all the time, but hardly ever at Doug; while he knows he's not special, Doug has always felt somewhat immune to Glenn's rage because he does the work of chopping iceberg and romaine and slicing and dicing vegetables without complaint. Even Merebeth seems affronted by the treatment, and she has never seemed to worry about anyone's emotional well-being in the kitchen.

Glenn himself seems to recognize his misstep, and after the storm of the dinner rush has ended, he thunks a meaty hand down on Doug's shoulder and apologizes. He's a big man, Glenn, with wizened crow's feet and a bulbous red nose. His hair has gone gray and is stringier than it used to be, and greasier; since Rhoda's vanishing, he seems to have shucked most normal human hygiene rituals and replaced them with drinking more Dewars. Doug accepts his apology but also acknowledges that he's been distracted and that he really was making too many mistakes, which he promises not to do again.

"We all make mistakes," Glenn says, voice wobbly. Doug wonders if Glenn has chosen someone to remember. Perhaps a family member, a brother or sister, maybe one of his wife's kin, someone close who could at least become aware of the loss he's trudging through. If nothing else, Doug doesn't have to navigate the complications and emotional ravages of knowing that someone so close like Rion is suddenly gone. He tries to picture Rion plucked into the sky, vanishing into nowhere, and he feels a sour taste in his mouth.

When he clocks out, he decides to be bold and he sends Rion a message: *Can I bring you anything?* He doesn't expect a quick response, but one comes fast: *Anything?* Doug writes: *Yes, anything.* And Rion responds: *How about a milkshake?*

Doug sucks in a breath. He thinks of Lauren, how she cast him off after their post-milkshake encounter. But as he settles into his car Doug tells himself this is different, that Rion, having not been dissipated into the ether by the vanishings, isn't going anywhere.

There aren't many ice cream places in Thomasville besides the Dairy Queen on the edge of town, but north of the downtown square, hidden in a shopping center dominated by a Walmart Supercenter and a gas station that charges ten cents a gallon less than the places near campus, is a tiny kiosk-sized building that sells the best soft serve Doug has ever tasted. Earl's Swirls, the place is called, and it's run by a rotating staff of pimply high school students—never an Earl, as far as Doug can tell—that stare longingly out the walk-up window on balmy nights, probably dreaming of parties and pot and illicit bottles of schnapps and beer. A plastic tip jar sits next to the cash register inside the sliding window through which the kids pass shakes and ice cream cones, and Doug always makes sure to stuff in a few bills even if it takes them upwards of ten minutes to complete his orders, which aren't always right but are always delicious: the ice cream is thick and rich and tastes of cream and fat, the kind of delectable treat that makes him feel the need, the next day, to chuff through more time on the treadmill or to finish an extra set of burpees or jump squats to burn off the caloric density.

He orders a pair of plain vanilla milkshakes from the sleepy-eyed blonde girl working the window. She flashes him a braces-filled smile as she takes his credit card, and her smile grows when he pre-emptively tosses a five into the woefully-empty tip jar. She pulls two of the large paper cups even though he's ordered a pair of mediums, an upgrade she doesn't mention when she hands them and a pair of plastic-wrapped straws to Doug. She tells him to have a good night, and he says for her to do the same, and then he's back in the car.

The world seems dead-set against Doug getting to Rion's apartment fast; even though traffic is light on the main thoroughfare, a state highway that ribbons down to one lane in either direction as it swirls through the center of Thomasville, bordered by dollar stores shuttered for the night and fast food joints beaming out their harsh fluorescent lighting, he hits every light as it turns red. Doug can practically feel the milkshakes turning to soup in the cupholders. He eventually passes the McClain campus, abandoned for the summer, the pathways along the edge of the quad illuminated by lampposts that make Doug think of the Victorian era.

The Blue Apartment parking lot is jammed with cars, but Doug manages to find a single open spot, squeezing his car in between a gargantuan F-150 with a bent fender and the dumpster, which reeks of rotting vegetable matter and stale beer with an undercurrent of cat litter. He plucks up the milkshakes, paper cups sweaty and slick, and takes the stairs up to Rion's apartment two at a time. As soon as he knocks he hears a, "Come in!" and then he struggles to turn the knob but manages without dropping either of the shakes.

The apartment is an icebox, the air conditioning pummeling the room. He finds Rion curled up on one of the couches, covered in blankets, his midnight-blue comforter dragged from his bed along with another quilt that Doug vaguely recognizes from the roommate's bed.

"Jesus," Doug says.

"Hi," Rion says, voice croaky and seared as if he's not drunk any water in days.

Doug sits down on the empty second sofa and sets the milkshakes on the table, sliding one close to Rion. "It's freezing in here," he says.

"Sorry," Rion says, sniffling. "I've got the chills but I'm also hot. I probably shouldn't have had you come in. I don't want to get you sick."

"I have a robust immune system."

All throughout grade school and high school, when influenza and strep and whatever other viral and bacterial junk burned its way through his gross classmates, Doug found himself in perfect health. While other students were out for weeks at a time he felt perfectly fresh; in eighth grade, he won the perfect attendance award for the third year in a row, a streak that would have been four years if his father hadn't made him miss a day of school in fifth grade for bring-your-kid-to-work day. Doug didn't take particular pride in his ability to remain healthy into college, when one particularly nasty strand of the flu ran through his dormitory freshman year and infected practically all of campus; his classes were half empty, some cancelled because his professors were ravaged by sore throats and throbbing headaches and terrible nausea. Through it all Doug remained a stalwart, taking up his usual seat in his classes and turning everything in on time. His reputation got around, and kids from his economics lecture started asking to borrow his notes; his history classmates wanted to study with him, and the kids in his American literature class wanted to know what hints about the take-home midterm their professor had dropped during the pseudo-pandemic.

"Have you gone to a doctor?" Doug says.

"It's the flu."

"In July?"

Rion makes what appears to be a shrugging motion. He sniffles, then extends a hand from his mound of blankets for the milkshake.

"I'm not sure dairy is good for the flu," Doug says.

"I don't care."

"Okay."

Rion slurps, and Doug is sure it's his imagination that color enters Rion's cheeks and he seems to stop trembling for a second. He sits up straight, letting the blankets fall from around his shoulders. Rion isn't wearing a shirt, and his skin is slicked with perspiration, like he's just run several miles at the height of noontime sun and heat.

"Good as new," Doug says with a smile.

"Perfect," Rion says, shaking his cup. "Thanks for bringing it."

"My pleasure. I feel like I should have done more."

Rion shrugs. "You're not my mother."

"Don't have to be a mom to care."

Rion shivers and pulls one of the blankets around him like a serape.

"I should go," Doug says.

"Please don't."

"You need rest."

"I've been resting for two days. I think I'm going insane."

"Okay," Doug says. They're silent again. The television is on, a Cardinals game muted. West coast, it must be, because it's only the bottom of the second. They watch for a while. Doug finds it strange, not hearing anything: the announcers' babbling brook voices, the thrum of the crowd, the spike of shrieking fans when a ball is belted deep or a strikeout swinging ends a tense inning. He glances at Rion, whose attention is fixed on the television, his skin swimming with the reflected light of the tv. The glowy light makes Rion's face unfamiliar, weird, otherworldly, accentuating the upturn of his button nose, gathering the swoop of his hair, which, despite his dishevelment, is parted hard on the right side. His cheekbones are carves of rock bulging from his face.

Doug wants to say a lot of things. He has questions. He has feelings that he wants to let out, like the carbonation in a soda desperate to be released. But he can't cut through the silence; every time he opens his mout, his lips feel dry, Sahara-cracked, as if it is him, and not Rion, who is blitzed by illness. Every time Rion moves, shifting his weight as he grabs his milkshake, or coughs, or clears his phlegm-laden throat, or releases a small groan or a loud shiver, Doug swallows whatever is coming to mind.

"You're not drinking your shake," Rion says.

Doug looks at it. "I'm not sure I really want it."

"You kidding? They're delicious."

"I know that."

Rion smiles. "No one else ever goes to Earl's."

"I go there all the time," Doug says. "Here." He pushes his toward

Rion.

"You sure?"

Doug nods, and Rion barely hesitates to grab it up. Doug imagines that Rion's appetite has been torn to shreds by being sick; whenever his mom or dad fell ill, they didn't ever want to eat anything, not even the most innocuous bowl of low-sodium chicken broth. In what feels like a single fell swoop, Rion has sucked down half of Doug's milkshake.

"Good old vanilla," he says. "Everyone I know likes fancy flavors, but for me it's the classics."

"Me, too," Doug says.

They sit in a fresh silence and, bloated on dairy product, Rion lays down. Soon enough, he's asleep, his cocooned body rising and falling with the rhythms of slumber. Doug doesn't care much about the baseball game, so he decides he should slip out, but before he goes, he steps carefully over to Rion and watches him sleep. He leans down and presses his lips to Rion's blazing hot forehead, telling himself that at least some of that warmth is for him. Then he lets himself out, shutting the door quietly behind him. Doug takes in a long, deep breath, then exhales slowly. Something settles in his chest, pleasant and tight, and he smiles the entire trip back to his house.

◆

When Rion returns to Lake | Drive exactly a week after their night in the water, Doug is already in the middle of prep, his station a mess of tomatoes and pepperoncini and artichoke hearts that need breaking down; the ingredients for the home-made balsamic dressing sit in their tubs, ready to be whisked together before the dinner rush. Doug and Rion have sent texts since Doug went to Rion's apartment, innocuous garbage, Rion starting with a thanks for the milkshakes, Doug saying no problem and asking how Rion was feeling, Rion saying better, slowly better, Doug saying that's good, I'm glad, Rion saying thanks, and then everything kept stalling out. Doug went to the gym and the restaurant neither seeing nor hearing from Rion at all.

When Rion walks into the kitchen, dolled up in his crisp white shirt, apron already tied around his waist, copper hair combed for the first time in days, Doug hopes that the warmth he feels in his center isn't exposed in a red blast in his cheeks. Carter is pulling plates from the expo window, and when he turns past Doug he doesn't say anything. He nods at Rion as he passes, offers a quick, "Welcome back," and is gone. Rion clocks in and smiles at Doug.

"You look better," Doug says as he corrals a Roma tomato that doesn't want to be diced.

"I feel better. Must have been the milkshakes."

"That was days ago."

"It kickstarted my road to recovery."

"If you say so."

Rion places a hand on Doug's shoulder and says, "I do," before he leaves the kitchen. Doug scans the room. Cynthia has her back to him, and Merebeth is squinting at a ticket that's just printed on the wheel. The only person looking in his direction is Satiya, who is macerating blackberries. She gives him a coy smile and a tilt of the head when their eyes meet. He turns back to his vegetables.

The night progresses in normal enough fashion. Wendy and Merebeth get in yelling matches with Timothie and then Evan over who is responsible for fucked up steaks that guests want recooked. Twice plates go out with the wrong sides, coleslaw where whipped potatoes or a baker belong. Doug makes no mistakes, and Glenn makes a show of expressing his gratitude for Doug's good work at the end of the night. He's still bloated and boozy, but Doug thinks that maybe Glenn looks a little better, not quite so red-eyed and despondent. It's strange, Doug thinks, how such massive pain can blunt itself quickly. But then he also thinks that he's probably wrong; Glenn is just figuring out how to hide his hurt rather than actually recovering from it.

The kitchen quiets down. Doug takes his time finishing his prep work for the morning in the hopes that Rion will appear, but even though there are almost no orders coming in, he's nowhere to be found. Donny is on back station for side work and Carter on expo, meaning that Rion has the front station, out of Doug's sight. Unless he's the one to gather the last wave of freshly-washed silverware from Cynthia to roll, Rion will have no real reason to come back to the kitchen again until he clocks out, and that he could do from the front of house. It pains Doug to think that he might not come by to at least say hello again. Or goodbye. Or anything.

But then, as if Doug has conjured him from the ether, Rion steps into the kitchen as Timothie swishes his way out. Merebeth has magically disappeared into the walk-in refrigerator with Wendy to count something or other, and Cynthia is dragging a heap of trash to the dumpster. The only other person in the kitchen is Satiya, who is scrubbing out her stand mixer by hand. He glances at her, but she is singularly devoted to swiping away every clinging bit of the cheesecake mixture she produced that afternoon.

Rion already has his apron off, curled into a tight package of fabric and straws.

"Hi," Doug says.

"Hi." Rion smiles, eyes squinty.

"Done?"

"Yep. You?"

Doug looks at his station: he could easily get away with saying that he is ready to clock out; no one would notice (servers on the day shift make their own salads and are constantly leaving the station looking like a bomb has gone off in a garden, messes Doug cleans up himself without complaint).

"Close enough."

Rion smiles. "I'll wait for you."

"Where?"

Rion laughs. "The bar. Where else?"

Doug wants to say, *Anywhere else*, but instead he nods and says, "Okay."

A few minutes later Doug punches out on the Point of Sales and pulls off his apron, dumping it into the basket full of dirtied linens; unlike the servers, who are on their own when it comes to removing stains and streaks from their clothes, Glenn pays for the kitchen staff to have theirs washed and dried, and each of them has a stack near dry storage they can pull from at the beginning of each shift. Doug is grateful for this, because it reduces by a seeming order of magnitude how much he reeks of dressing and wilting greens every night.

He steps out of the kitchen like he's entering a different universe. Where the floors of the kitchen are obnoxious red as if pretending to be terra cotta, the floors of the Lake | Drive dining room are rich chocolate hardwood. The walls are soft eggshell white. Just past the swinging kitchen doors is the back drink station, where two computers flank a steel countertop covered in stacked pint glasses. To the left is the entryway to the bar and a view of the Perry's host stand, and to the right is the maw that leads into the dining room and the bump-out. Doug feels thrummy with nerves; he can hear the servers, seated at the bar, laugh-

127

ing about their demanding tables while they count their tips and drink their after-shift cocktails. Angela comes barreling around the corner just as Doug is about to walk out and nearly plows into him. She's carrying a stack of emptied plates and Doug manages to leap out of the way at the last second.

"Jesus Christ!" she says, stopping in her tracks. Of all the servers, Angela is the most mysterious to Doug because she is, in many ways, his mirror image: where he's the one boy in the back, she's the one woman in the front. Angela has always treated him with professional respect, never yelling at him for an extra side of dressing or castigating him if he should accidentally leave the red onions on a house salad where they've been requested to be left off. She comes across as cold sometimes, her voice monotone when she makes a request at the expo line, but he knows that she makes excellent money; Glenn wouldn't have her as the dining room closer if she was robotic with the literati and upper crust of Thomasville.

She looks him over, as though having trouble placing him, Doug, a kitchen peon, as he stands on the outskirt of the fanciful dining room. Then Angela smiles and glances toward the bar, where Doug can hear Donny telling some kind of lewd joke, eliciting guffawing laughter from Andrew and Carter.

"Good luck out there," she says, then swivels past him.

Doug takes a breath and walks into the dining room.

Carter is still laughing at Donny's punchline, actually wiping a tear from one of his eyes. Andrew and Andre are drinking draft beers, looking like reflections of one another with their pint glasses at their lips. Timothie is still on the clock, but he's leaning against the bar. He notices Doug first, standing up straight and smirking at him like Doug is some pathetic freshman dweeb in a high school lunch room looking to sit with the popular upperclassmen. Rion is sitting facing Timothie, or at least that's what Doug thinks at first, but then he sees that Rion is looking beyond him, out the wall of windows toward the darkness of the night. He's gripping a rocks glass full of ice and clear liquid: perhaps vodka, perhaps Sprite, perhaps both. When he sees Doug, he stands and grins.

"Gotta go, guys," Rion says. Andre, sitting nearest, turns to look at Doug, and suddenly all of the servers are staring at him. Doug's hands dangle at his sides, and he doesn't know what to do with them. He makes a fist of his left and shoves the right in his pocket, reaching for his car keys.

"Hot date?" Donny says. Evan, behind the bar, blinks at Doug and looks at Rion.

"Hotter than you can imagine," Rion says. He plucks up his apron from the bar and drains his drink, nodding toward Evan.

"On the house tonight," Evan says.

Doug can practically see everyone's eyes bug out; Evan never gives drinks away for free. He told Doug, once, that if a bartender gave away one free drink, that was game over: the benefacted would come to expect such handouts all the time; if you could slide a free rum and coke down the bar one night, why not every night? If a Budweiser could be uncapped at no cost once, why not in perpetuity? It was enough, Evan thought, that Glenn had greenlit him charging half for beers and cocktails for the employees. Wasn't it? Doug had nodded.

So naturally everyone's attention snaps-to at Evan's gift to Rion.

Doug feels his face flaring red. His body temperature only seems to rise when Rion snatches his right wrist and pulls it from its pocket and then threads his own fingers through Doug's. The Lake | Drive boys practically gape. If Doug has figured out any one thing, it's that while these boys are willing and ready to go home with one another and are happy to show it through ass-slaps and flirtation and other ridiculous displays that Doug can't fathom being comfortable giving or receiving, this, Rion's hand wound through his, is something else, something different: there's an intimacy here, an emotional gesture that goes beyond physical pleasure.

Doug says nothing. He wishes he could look all of them in the eye, asshole Donny and quiet Carter, Andre and doofy Andrew, proud and confident Timothie, kind-enough Evan. But he keeps his eyes down, on Rion's hand in his, even as Rion leads him from the restaurant, out into the night, where, when the door closes behind them, Rion starts laughing, his grip on Doug's hand tightening, his body turning to Doug's to throw his free arm over Doug's shoulder so they're face-to-face. Rion kisses him, a hard peck on the cheek. He laughs again, and then his mouth is on Doug's and he's still laughing. When he lets Doug go, Rion actually spins around in a quick circle then slaps his thighs and says, "Did you see the looks on their faces?"

All Doug can do is nod. The entryway to Lake | Drive is covered in a burgundy awning, reminiscent of old New York hotels, narrow and long and decorated, on the inner side, by strings of fairy lights like those garnishing the gazebo at The Drive. Rion's face is illuminated by the lights, his eyes' natural blue tinged with their gold. His smile is rich and deep and his lips glossed with moisture. Doug trembles just so, not only because he can sense that tonight things will happen that have never happened before but because he feels seen, visible for the first time. While the rest of the world may have forgotten about so much, he can see in Rion's eyes that he, Doug, is someone that at least this person, this one, will not ever forget.

PART FOUR

YOU

THERE *is pleasure in change. There is pleasure in watching them find themselves and one another. It blooms through your chest, washes between your ears like water sloshing, an ocean against the cave wall of your skull. It settles in your throat, a pleasant, raw ache.*

Seeing them all doing and doing and doing, finding and finding and finding.

This is the new world you have built, have wanted to build. Success blossoms like a bloodstain, and you feel the first tickles of something that surprises you: pride, joy, like you've given birth, not just to a world, but to the wonders within it.

CYNTHIA

CYNTHIA doesn't like to be nosy, but she can't help it in this case.

It's not her fault that she was outside. Maybe, okay, she was taking her sweet time with the trash, longer than was necessary to toss the night's most recent detritus into the dumpster (sloth, for which she promises to ask forgiveness). It's not her fault she saw Rion and Doug practically prancing across the parking lot, hand in hand. It was pitch-dark outside, the Lake | Drive marquee already off—Glenn has it set on a timer to click off at nine-thirty every weeknight; he keeps it blazing later on weekends—but she could see in their movements that this wasn't just another hookup. They were laughing, practically giggling like the girls Cynthia had hated in grade school (wrath, which was very hard to let go of, especially when Heather Kiting stuck bubble gum to Cynthia's scalp, which required a terrible haircut that took a year to recover from). She watched Doug and Rion separate at one of their cars, but not before kissing at the rear bumper, as if they were saying goodbye forever; it looked like something out of a romantic comedy. If it had been anyone besides Doug, she'd have thought it nauseating. But as he climbed into the passenger seat and then the car disappeared into the night, she found herself smiling.

Now, she stares.

Doug is at the salad station, finishing his chopping and straining and dicing and stocking before the dinner rush. The bump-out is reserved tonight, some complex niçoise salad on the prix fixe, so Doug is working fast for the first seating at six. Cynthia's station is largely empty, the first wave of early diners having barely polished off their appetizers; she's got a half-full rack that she could send shooting through the Hobart but little else. Cynthia doesn't want to look unbusy, because someone will come up with something beyond the scope of her job description for her to do. Last week, during an unusually dead night, Merebeth made her dole out bags of uncooked pasta in dry storage and label them all with the date and seal them with tape. Cynthia couldn't bring herself to say no, nor could she mount some excuse, so she got to work without complaint.

She leaves the dish station, wiping her hands on her apron even though they're clean.

Cynthia pulls her travel-size bottle of extra strength Jergens from her pocket and dobs some on her palm and rubs it around, greasing both sides of her hands and the spaces between her fingers. She's still rubbing when she approaches the salad station and says, "Need any help?"

Doug looks at her like she's accused him of murder.

"You just look a little disarrayed?"

"I don't think that's a word," Doug says. The station is a mess of potatoes and shallots. Cynthia can smell the tuna Merebeth seared this afternoon.

"Okay, how about 'in disarray.'"

"I'm fine."

"I'm just here to help."

Doug stares at her as if he can read her mind, knows that what she really wants is the scoop on him and Rion. But he holds out a steel bowl and says, "I guess I could use a hand with the dressing."

She spends a few minutes chopping thyme and whisking salt, pepper, and mustard into olive oil. Doug is silent, acting as though she's not even there. His brow is sweaty, a droplet of perspiration threatening to drip into the haricots verts. Cynthia watches him when she's finished with the dressing. If anything monumental has happened to him, he doesn't show it; Doug's body language is the same as always, full of rabid tension. His shoulders are always hitched, as if he's been frozen mid-shrug. She understands that they carry something on them, something no one else can see. We all do, Cynthia thinks: we all have something no one else understands, something that drags at us, pulls at our skulls. She thinks of Mama, of Papa, of her not-quite brother and sister. She thinks of the jealousy she felt at the way Rion and Doug embraced, how the sour deadly sin of envy crept through her body, tickling at her throat. How she tamped it down, told herself she was just happy for these boys who'd found something that most everyone spends their life searching for.

Finally, when the salads are done, Doug looks to her and says, "Thanks for the help."

She's about to tell him it's no problem when Rion comes bursting into the kitchen. The tension and weight in Doug's shoulders vanishes. They haven't even spoken, yet suddenly Doug seems taller, his face brighter, as if a cherubim has lit him from within. Cynthia feels that same stirring, but this time she welcomes it, basking in the second-hand feeling of unadulterered adoration. Love, she thinks.

Cynthia is not so prideful as to tell Doug of her role in the events that have clearly unfolded between him and Rion. How, the day she first saw the way Doug looked at him, she waited until Rion was dropping off some plates and soup bowls and stepped as quickly as she could from the dish pit and, surprising him, grabbed his wrist. His eyes went wide, but she started by saying thank you, which relaxed him. She told him how much she appreciated that he was always careful to stack dishes with like dishes, instructions she knew that every server had been given but most of them ignored (she did not name names, but everyone knew that Donny and Timothie were particularly scattershot with their platters and bowls, creating ridiculous contemporary art sculptures out of mis-matched porcelain). With Rion relaxed, she nodded toward Doug, who was busy with a pair of cobb salads and said, "He's the same way."

Rion had glanced toward Doug. Cynthia tightened her grip on his wrist and whispered to herself, so quiet only she could hear thanks to the din of frying foods and clanging cookware, "He likes you, he loves you, he wants you to want him."

After she released Rion's wrist, she wished she'd said something more impressive, more meaningful, but regret, though not one of the sins, was also not a state of mind she wished to fall into.

Cynthia returns to the dish station and busies herself spraying down the chute leading to the Hobart while still paying attention to the way Rion and Doug interact. Rion is good at this: most people might think that nothing is unusual or different between them, because he's careful to keep his voice steady, his mouth purled in a normal-enough smile. But Cynthia can see the way he leans in toward Doug in a different way now. He doesn't reach out and touch Doug, but Cynthia can see how the desire is there, unspoken. She smiles as she finishes spraying out the pesky corners of her steel enclosure, where shreds of lettuce and gristle like to pack themselves away. An avoidance of sloth, even if she's really just giving her hands something to do while she watches the boys interact. Carter comes in through the swinging doors and empties a pair of pint glasses full of ice and leftover soda and then tosses the steins into the glass rack. He passes Doug and Rion by without a second look.

There it is again, that steam-up of pride, of her knowing something she's sure no one else knows. Cynthia takes a long breath, trying to drain the beating feeling from behind her eyes. But she really can't help herself. She feels like a matchmaker, that this burgeoning thing is her doing. That her words, while not bringing back any memories, have done something far more important, far more useful. She tells herself that it's okay to be proud of herself as long as she keeps it to herself: no one will ever know the role she's played. As Rion leaves the kitchen, she nods to herself. Yes, quiet pride can be alright, she decides, especially if in the service of bringing happiness to someone else. Mama would agree, Cynthia thinks, even if she has no real reason to believe so. But that's the point of belief, of faith: it hinges on the self, the fire inside, reliant on no evidence except a feeling. Cynthia watches Doug move about the salad station and feels it, this thrilling flame that she has done something right, something important, something that will last.

WENDY

CARLA will not leave Wendy alone. Each night after work Wendy, set upon sprawling out on her couch with a beer and tumbling into a light doze before rousing herself in the middle of the night to slink to her bedroom, instead finds herself in her sister's orbit. When she checks her phone first thing after clocking out, there is always a message, a demand that they hang out. Carla always has a new reason: she's bored, her plans got cancelled, she met some guy but he turned out to be a total weirdo and she needs to debrief, she's suddenly remembered someone else who has vanished from her life. These demands grate on Wendy's nerves, make her grit her teeth until her jaw hurts, but she feels as if she cannot say no.

On the one hand, giving Carla her memory back has made her needy.

On the other, she seems to have finally figured Wendy out.

In the immediate aftermath of Wendy taking her sister's hand and telling her to remember, Carla went briefly deaf and dumb, as if she'd been clobbered on the back of the head with a shovel, and Wendy wondered if she'd done it wrong—though Doug had given her no indication there was a right or wrong way to do it—and was going to end up with a comatose sibling, or a sister struck by dementia or something. But then Carla shuddered, a whole-body convulsion like she was having a grand mal seizure—another thing Doug hadn't prepared her for—and her eyes opened wide.

"Whoa," Carla said, and then stared at Wendy for a long time.

Wendy hadn't been sure how to proceed. She'd turned on the television, wading through crappy local news until she found coverage of something that she knew had been altered. Carla grabbed her tight by the arm when she saw that one of her favorite movie stars had been replaced in his recent blockbuster. She groaned as if their parents were divorcing all over again.

Wendy said, "I know."

They'd stayed up half the night. Carla scrolled through her phone, hitting every social media site on which she had an account—which for Carla was most of them—sending out a spray of lamentation over every person who seemed to have been wiped out of the world; the results were much worse for Carla than for Wendy, because she, unlike Wendy, had made the effort to retain her connections with high school and college friends.

Wendy, by contrast, has never cared about those old ties, even to her former roommate, a rainbow-haired girl named Liesel who declared her lesbianism to Wendy when they first met, as if she was simply sharing her major or hometown. Liesel and Carla never met—this was fresh in Wendy and Carla's separation, when they still sort of hated each other—and Wendy isn't exactly sad to have kept it that way. Liesel was the one who first gave Wendy any kind of sexual direction, not in that she hit on Wendy or tried to make something romantic out of nothing; after six months of living in tight close quarters, Liesel looked at Wendy one afternoon while they were both studying and said, "Do you think you might be asexual?"

"That I might be what?" Wendy had said, which had led to an hour-long lecture from Liesel about the colorful breadth of the LG-

BTQIA spectrum.

Tonight, Wendy finds a trio of text messages from Carla: the first a feelers greeting, a seemingly-innocuous *how's work?* that's actually the most annoying of the three because Carla should know that Wendy can't take the time to answer while she's a dozen dinner tickets deep, trying to avoid overcooking an expensive side of beef or making sure she's got the right kind of potato accompanying the right sirloin burger; the second is a declaration of Carla's boredom—literally *I'm so bored*—despite having McClain co-workers who would surely make a trek to one of the garbage bars if Carla would just pick up the phone and ask; and third, finally, *Please come over; I'll make margs!*

Wendy appreciates the properly-utilized semi-colon. She also appreciates that Carla is actually making use of the Christmas gift Wendy bought for her last holiday season, a pricey Margaritaville Bahamas drink mixer that takes up half of Carla's counterspace but has gotten good mileage, Carla experimenting with pineapple coladas, raspberry daiquiris, sex on the beach slushies, and, of course, Montezuma-nasty margaritas.

Despite the throb in her feet and the fact that she reeks of fryer oil and raw beef, Wendy, after clocking out, drives over to Carla's. Halfway there, she receives another text, her phone rattling the change in her cupholder. As she idles at a stoplight, she checks it: *Please, Wendy.* Wendy frowns; Carla doesn't write *please* in her text messages. So Wendy pushes the gas pedal a little harder when the light shifts green. She risks etching over the speed limit by an extra two miles per hour, and she takes the stairs up to Cynthia's unit two at a time despite the knotted exhaustion she feels in her chest and hamstrings.

When her sister throws open the door, she already has a frosted glass in hand. Carla thrusts it toward Wendy. The liquid inside is a neon green and reminds Wendy of radioactive waste. Cynthia's face is a boggling mix of excitement and bizarre discomfort. She lets out a weird laugh when Wendy frowns at the drink.

"I may have overdone it on mixer. But I balanced it out with extra tequila!"

Wendy frowns and takes the drink, which is buttressed by a gargantuan pink paper umbrella so large she has to pluck it from the glass before she can suck from the teal reusable straw embedded into the icy floes. Cynthia scooches out of the way so Wendy can enter, but she keeps staring at her with a maniacal smile on her face.

And then Wendy sees why: their mother is sitting on the couch.

It's not that Wendy dislikes her mother. She certainly doesn't hate her. There's no animus over the divorce; Wendy was already out of the house, a college freshman when her parents broke the news, calling her up one Sunday afternoon while she was nursing a hangover following the PKG luau, to which one of her hallmates dragged her to at two in the afternoon. They spoke to her like they were trying to calm a wild animal, as though Wendy might combust, screaming and wailing at them over the phone. She was pretty sure they were disappointed that she wasn't more distraught.

"Hi, Mom," Wendy says.

Her mother looks great. Wendy hasn't seen her in a while, but she's pretty sure that she's got the richest tan she's ever had; it looks sprayed-on, which would probably be safer than the alternatives. Cancer runs in the family, having taken out both of Wendy's maternal grandparents (granddad: pancreatic; grandmom: breast). But it's not just the color of her mother's skin that appears radiant. Wendy's mother has always been plagued by wrinkles around her eyes and mouth, the lines appearing when she was in her late thirties and growing deeper every year. But now her mother's skin is perfectly smooth, as if she's been airbrushed. Her hair, which is usually a chestnut brown that she keeps bobbed at her shoulders, is midnight black and dangles halfway down her back. If Wendy didn't know any better, she'd think her mother was wearing a wig.

"Hey sweetheart." Her mother has her own glass, half-empty, the pink umbrella tucked closed so it looks like a bulbous antenna. She doesn't bother standing to greet Wendy. Instead, she stretches out like a cat, back arched against the arm of Cynthia's sofa. "How was work?"

Wendy raises an eyebrow at Cynthia, trying to convey *Why didn't you tell me Mom would be here?* But Cynthia smiles, crooked, and slurps from her own drink. Wendy rolls her eyes and drinks—the heavy-handed tequila and sugar clear her sinuses right away—and turns to her mom.

"It was fine. Busy."

"Still firing away in the kitchen, huh?"

Wendy clamps her mouth shut. Ever since divorcing their father, their mother has become something of a second-wave feminist, though as far as Wendy knows she hasn't actually read any theory. She doesn't think Wendy is improving the state of womankind by working in a kitchen despite Wendy's explanation that the restaurant industry is male-dominated, particularly on the back-of-house side. Sure, there are exceptions, but what Wendy is doing, especially at Lake | Drive with its all-female kitchen staff (Doug excepted) is important. It's meaning-ful. To her, at least, and isn't that what feminism is all about? Her mother just scoffs and makes jokes about wishing Wendy had become a physicist or something.

Before Wendy can take a seat, Cynthia grips her arm and says, "Speaking of which, can you help me in the kitchen for a second?"

"Be right back," Wendy says to their mother and allows Cynthia to drag her out of the living room.

"What's going on?" Wendy says.

"Shh," Cynthia says. She's holding Wendy's bicep. "She'll hear you."

"She'll hear me what?"

"Something's wrong with her, Wendy."

Wendy blinks. "So she had her hair done. And a little skin work."

"It's not just that."

Cynthia goes on to explain: their mother is different, somehow. "She doesn't even remember Roberto."

Wendy takes a deep breath. "Well, it's not entirely surprising that someone close to us disappeared." For a moment, Wendy feels a brief spike of shame: where Cynthia spent time rooting through her social sphere and the pop culture universe for losses, Wendy didn't even think to check in on their mother, whose long-time boyfriend, the first man she dated after splitting up with their father, has, according to Cynthia, vanished.

"It's not just that," Cynthia is saying. "She's all weird. Like a different person."

Wendy takes a step back to look into the living room. Their mother doesn't seem to have processed their absence; she's relaxed, eyes closed, hands tented on her stomach in a dome of fingers.

"She looks happy," Wendy says.

"That's the thing," Carla says. "Since when is she happy?"

Wendy takes a drink, the tequila a pleasant burn in her throat. She hates to admit it, but Carla is right. Ever since the divorce, even after meeting Roberto and seeming to fall in love again—their mother used that phrase, *in love*, many times, to describe her relationship—she was always muted, as though true happiness had been stripped from her by

144

some fairy tale curse. Discontent always seemed to sit on her shoulders like a nasty, invisible homunculus, never quite letting her relax or fully enjoy anything. Certainly never in the way she seems to be zenning out on Carla's couch at the moment.

"Okay," Wendy says, trying to choose her words carefully. "You're right. But does different have to be bad?"

Carla bites her lip. "I guess not. It's just strange. She's, like, not our mother anymore."

"Again," Wendy says. "Is that necessarily so bad?"

Carla blinks, and Wendy sees that her sister is on the verge of tears. Her grip on Wendy's arm relaxes. "I wish I hadn't remembered. I wish I didn't know the truth."

Wendy understands: before Wendy gave Carla her memory, this transformed version of their mother was the mother that Carla remembered. If erasing Roberto has sent her mother onto this new, different path, Carla now knows both paths. Wendy realizes that the Lake | Drive staff didn't just remember the true past: they also didn't inherit a false one. After all, every one of the people who has vanished was replaced in some way. Although Glenn doesn't have a new wife, Rhoda has been supplanted in the memories of everyone who knew her except for him and his staff. Unlike Timothie and Doug and Cynthia and the rest, everyone else in the world has been sent flying down a new trajectory. And the people that the Lake | Drive staff awaken—to use Satiya's word—now have dual memories and, possibly, dual personalities.

Carla picks up a kitchen towel and dabs at her face, which is smeary with tears. Wendy doesn't know what to say. In the living room, their mother lets out an, "Oh, girls? Where are my girls?" Her voice is singsongy and foreign, as though her body has been taken over by some alien parasite.

145

"It's going to be fine," Wendy says. Carla shakes her head, and Wendy doesn't say so, but she agrees: Carla is right. Wendy is wrong. The world is turned upside down in more ways than she can know. More than anyone, even the Lake | Drive staff, will ever know.

Carla, straightening, blows out a breath and checks her face against the chrome of her sink. Then, before Wendy can say anything, Carla is dragging her back into the living room, where their foreign mother is waiting.

SATIYA

SATIYA is pulled from sleep by the vibration of her cell phone. She groans into the darkness and rubs her eyes. Without looking at the phone, she knows that her mother is calling. When she picks up the phone, she lets out a second groan: four-fifteen in the morning. She was planning to sleep in, maybe go for a hike at Hundred Hills Park north of town; the weather is supposed to be unseasonably cool, and although there will be crowds, she could use some fresh air. The last time she spent any real time outdoors was the last time she worked The Drive, helping Timothie wine and dine the mayor who had not been mayor in the minds of anyone at the restaurant.

She's tempted not to answer, but the first few times she missed her mother's middle of the night calls Satiya felt wracked with guilt. After all, she was the reason her mother kept calling in the first place: every time she discovered something else that was different in her life, she suffered an acute bout of insomnia, and the only person she could talk to, the only person who could soothe her into sleep, was Satiya.

"Hello Mama," Satiya says. Her voice is scratchy and dry; she heaves herself out of bed and pads through the dark, her phone pinched between her ear and shoulder. In the dark, she nearly trips over her work shoes as she navigates the living room en route to the kitchen for a glass of water.

"Louisa is gone!"

"Louisa?"

"You know," Amah says, voice trembling. "The woman who used to do my hair."

"When I was in grade school?"

"Yes! Her!"

Satiya fills a glass. She tries to gather herself as she drinks, as if the water is full of ideas for how to navigate her mother's newest discovery. As far as Satiya can remember, her mother hasn't been to the salon where Louisa worked in over a decade, having changed her hairdresser when the family moved into a bigger house in a bigger and better neighborhood with better salons with better stylists and products. But Satiya knows not to point this out; it will only make Amah more upset.

"How did you figure this out?" Satiya says as she sets down the glass.

"I went by, of course. I asked for Louisa, and the woman at the check-in had no idea who I was talking about."

"Maybe she changed jobs. It's been a long time."

"They had no records of her. None! And then I went on Facebook and couldn't find her."

Satiya doesn't point out that there must be hundreds, maybe thousands, of Louisas, and she's guessing that Amah has no idea what Louisa's last name is, and it's possible that Louisa isn't even on Facebook.

"I'm sorry, Mama."

"I just don't know what to do."

"About Louisa?" Satiya says, but she knows that isn't what her mother means.

"About any of it! I keep discovering things, people that are gone. Things that are different. And, of course, I can't speak about it with your father."

"I know, Mama." Satiya feels a cold stab in her throat. Although she's glad her mother remembers Anlusia so that Satiya is no longer the only one who has to carry the woman's memory, she also feels sorrow for the toll that awakening has taken on her mother. She thinks of her own awakenings, how there was maybe an initial stab of hurt at recognizing that something she thought she knew about herself turned out to be incorrect. But how quickly those hurts had subsided, obscured by the new joys that came with discovering something new. With Amah, none of that joy is present: the only discoveries are of absence and change, transformations that only she, and her daughter, can reckon with.

"He seems so different," Amah whispers, and Satiya wonders where in the house her mother is sitting. She has tried to picture her mother gliding through the house in the dark staring at photographs, the paintings and objets d'art, sifting through her father's desk drawers, searching for signs of change. At Lake | Drive, Satiya listened while Wendy talked to Doug about her mother and her strange transformation as a result of the disappearance of her boyfriend, how it seemed like Wendy's mother had been rewritten, her personality transformed by the scrubbing of her memory. If nothing else, Satiya is glad that her mother hasn't undergone a similar metamorphosis, or if she did, she's been recouped to her old self as a result of Satiya granting her the gift of her memory, if one can even call it such; right now it certainly feels more like a curse.

"I understand, Mama," Satiya says. This, of course, is really a lie: Satiya has not gone home since awakening her mother, partly because of work but mostly because she's not sure how to interact with her father. She's barely spoken with anyone else who doesn't remember the truth, unless clerks at grocery stores and the bank count, which she's pretty sure they don't. The only people close to her are the kitchen girls at Lake | Drive and her mother, and they all, for better or worse, know the truth of the world. She tries to imagine being Amah, forced to live side-by-side with someone who doesn't know the world as she knows it. It makes her queasy.

"I should let you sleep. I'm sorry," Amah says.

"Please don't be," Satiya says, her voice low. "I'm sorry I made you remember."

Her mother tuts. "No, no, no. It must be this way. It must."

"But you're in pain."

"I am. But how could I be me if I didn't know the truth? I can't imagine life without Anlusia."

Satiya wants to say, but doesn't, that Anlusia is gone either way. Knowledge and memory don't bring someone back. But then she thinks that maybe they do. When people die, they are carried along by those they leave behind. If not for memory, none of us would exist, really.

"What if you wrote something about her?" Satiya says.

This makes Amah laugh, a sound that jolts Satiya; the warmth is real, a happy caterwaul spiking through her mother's grief. It's a relief to Satiya to hear it. She can picture her mother's throat, how her head tips back when she releases even the slightest of chuckles.

"I'm no writer. You know that."

"It doesn't have to be for anyone else. Maybe writing about the people whose disappearances you learn about will help you sleep."

"At least it would make me stop pestering my daughter."

"You're not a pest. You know that."

"Of course I am! You shouldn't be getting woken up by your crazy mother in the middle of the night."

Satiya thinks, but again doesn't say, that she's the one who's responsible for the waking up. If not for giving her mother her memory back,

150

they'd both be sound asleep right now.

"Maybe I will try writing," Amah says.

"If you do, tell me how it goes," Satiya says.

"Of course. Of course I will. I'm sorry."

Satiya's eyes hurt, tiredness weighing her down. "Please stop saying that. Why don't you try getting some sleep? Or some words in."

"Either or. In any case, please go back to bed. I'm sorry, Satiya."

"Mama."

Her mother giggles, and although Satiya is dead-tired, she smiles. She pours herself another glass of water and says goodbye before she drinks it down, letting its cool weight settle in her stomach, a gurgling mass that makes her feel like a buoy. If nothing else, hopefully she can keep her mother afloat.

MEREBETH

"**ARE** you sure about this?"

Glenn's office is tucked in a corner of the kitchen next to the dry goods pantry, where stacks of canned vegetables and fruits hide from the prying eyes of paying customers who would be shocked and appalled by the percentage of their "fresh ingredients" that have been sitting in preservatives for weeks. The room is barely bigger than a broom closet but has the freshest white paint in the kitchen, probably because the walls aren't battered by fryer grease and smoke on a daily basis. Inside, Glenn has stuffed two filing cabinets—it takes him ages, Merebeth knows, to throw out a single receipt—on one side of the room. The other holds a built-in desk home to a slow-going desktop computer and three shelves, all of which are crammed with binders of who knows what; Merebeth has never seen Glenn so much as touch one of them. The most impressive feat is that Glenn has somehow also jammed a large ergonomic chair into the room; it's the perfect size for being able to turn in a complete circle without whoever is seated there, almost always Glenn, whacking their shins and knees on the cabinets or the desk.

"I'm sure," Glenn says. He picks up his rocks glass—filled, Merebeth notices, with water—and takes a drink, ice tinkling against his teeth.

"But why?"

Glenn lets out a shuddering breath, as though he's trying not to cry. His eyes are bloodshot, and Merebeth isn't sure whether that's due to lack of sleep, too much drink, actual tears, or some combination thereof.

"I need some time."

Glenn won't meet her eye. She's seen the way the summer has destroyed him, ever since Rhoda's disappearance. He's never been warm and fuzzy, but he's also never been grating and nasty like he was with Doug. No one working at Lake | Drive expects to be patted on the back by Glenn or told how wonderful they are at their jobs, but they also know they can rely on his laughing at their mistakes, even if they're pricey (when she started, Merebeth managed to accidentally scorch a forty-dollar filet mignon; in response, rather than fire her, Glenn told her to eat two bites of it and then try again, and on her second attempt she seared it perfectly). He's never been in particularly great shape, but he's become more stoop-shouldered. His face is puffier, his voice rawer, like he spends his off-hours screaming or chain smoking.

They haven't talked about Rhoda, especially because Amy is still around. How to manage that elephant in the room, one that's only grown larger because not only did Amy not disappear, she now knows about the vanishings, too? Merebeth has heard the rest of the staff, particularly Doug and whoever else will talk to him, discuss whom they have given memories back to. For some of them, like Satiya, it sounds like things have gone sideways, her mother plagued by the knowledge she's gained. Others seem satisfied, the restitution of memory coming with no noticeable negative side effects. Being in that camp makes things challenging, especially around someone like Glenn, the only person at Lake | Drive who has directly had someone erased from the world.

But now he wants her to take over the restaurant while he's gone.

153

Gone being something different than Rhoda's gone, but still gone.

"I've never run a restaurant before," Merebeth says.

Glenn waves a hand in her direction, like a bear lazily swatting at her. "You basically run the kitchen. That's the hard part. The servers can take care of themselves. You just write up their schedules."

Merebeth purses her lips.

"Who else am I going to ask? Timothie?"

"I already get home late," Merebeth says, then feels immediate regret. Even though she hasn't mentioned Amy by name, Merebeth's wife hovers there, a ghost, the unstated point being that while Glenn has no one to go home to anymore, Merebeth does.

"We can hire another cook for the time being. Upgrade Wendy to leading the line while you do my job."

"My job is to cook food, Glenn. Not to corral a bunch of boys to do their side work or to sign delivery orders. I don't have any idea how payroll works."

"I can show you all of that," Glenn says, his voice shocking in how pleading it is. The whinging makes her stomach churn. Merebeth closes her eyes and takes a deep breath.

"I'm going to have to talk to Amy about it. When do you need an answer?"

"Sooner than later," Glenn says.

"Do you know where you'll go? For how long?"

Glenn shakes his head.

"Give me until tomorrow, okay?"

Glenn nods.

The kitchen at Lake | Drive is a weird place, windowless and lit by harsh fluorescents that are butter yellow thanks to the build-up of grease. The only indicator of the time is the clock above Doug's salad station, which is rolled back ten minutes so that no one gets too pissed when a late-night order comes through three minutes before close, a warped opposite of bar time. It's possible to see the wall of windows that look onto the lake if you're standing at just the right angle at the swinging doors leading to the back station. The only other egress with any natural light is the back door, where deliveries come in and garbage, and departing staff, go out.

All this to say that, when Merebeth leaves the office, she is discombobulated by the sunset streaming through the kitchen's back door, which Cynthia has propped open to make it easier for her to drag the trash out. Tonight's been slow: only a handful of tables even at seven, the dining room quiet enough that Satiya and Wendy are able to handle the line themselves while Merebeth and Glenn talk. When she returns to her place behind the expo window, Merebeth can feel Wendy's eyes on her, the question pursed on her lips. But Wendy says nothing.

Not, at least, until Glenn emerges from the office wearing one of the kitchen aprons, his hair held back by a blue-and-pink bandana. Wendy stares at him as he cinches the apron around his belly, the fabric straining, tight as a wetsuit. Merebeth says nothing, not even as Glenn saunters over to where she stands and plucks up a ticket that's printing off the spool. He turns to Wendy and says he's got an order for fried artichoke hearts and that he needs a chicken breast for a southwestern salad. She stares at him, open-mouthed.

He finally looks at Merebeth. "Go home. Talk to Amy. I'll handle this."

The look on Wendy's face makes Merebeth nearly crackle with laughter: her eyes are so big, she looks as if she's been electrocuted. Her mouth is a slit, and she looks at Glenn and Merebeth as if they're playing a practical joke.

Merebeth doesn't need to be told twice, especially when Glenn says he'll adjust her clock out time to a normal shift so she doesn't lose any pay, an announcement that makes Wendy look even more comical. As she peels off her apron, Merebeth says nothing but tries, with her eyes, to convey to Wendy that she will explain later. As she leaves, she passes Cynthia, who is pulling the empty trash can along as if it is a disobedient dog she is trying to hurry through an evening walk. If Cynthia thinks anything is amiss in Merebeth's early departure, she doesn't say so, waving and calling out a cheery goodbye.

Amy's response to having her memory back has been surprisingly pleasant, much as Merebeth had dreamed. Rather than freaking out, she's been amazed, bemused, and humored by the changes in the world. She's guffawed at the president, saying, "God, they really are basically all the same old man, aren't they?" She lamented the loss of their friendly neighbors and has slowly started to come around to the weirdness of Phil by comparison. Whenever she discovers a new change, she sends Merebeth a text, even when she knows Merebeth won't see it until hours later. When she discovered that her brother's girlfriend had vanished, she said, "Good riddance. She was a homophobic bitch."

All the lights are on in the house when Merebeth arrives, the glow through the blinds giving her a pleasant feeling in her chest. Sometimes she wishes she'd gone into a more traditionally-houred career, one whose work days end at five and the weekends are actually weekends rather than her busiest, most tiring days. Merebeth imagines her and Amy being able to travel, to escape the doldrums of Thomasville more often. She also knows that accepting Glenn's offer, while good for her long-term career trajectory, will mean moving further away from that wish.

She enters through the carport and is greeted by the loud blast of

90s music, one of the boy bands that Amy pretends to listen to ironically (Merebeth has caught her mouthing along enthusiastically to the lyrics with perfect accuracy). The house smells of berries and sugar, and she's a bit surprised to find Amy in the kitchen, hips twitching to the Backstreet Boys as she stirs a pot. The music is too loud for Amy to have heard Merebeth's entrance, and the window above the sink is fogged from her baking. Merebeth steps up behind Amy and sees fresh dough set into pie pans and the filling for a blackberry pie simmering in a sauté pan. When she wraps her wife in a hug, Amy shrieks, her body twitching with surprise.

"Jesus!" Amy turns to her, face suddenly red. "What are you doing? You scared me."

"I could ask you the same thing," Merebeth says. "Seeing you in the kitchen is a bit scary. Since when do you bake?"

Amy wipes her brow. She's wearing a gingham apron, checked red and white, and her hair is pulled back into a ponytail, showing off the flush of her cheeks. "I wanted to try something new. To surprise you."

"Well, I am surprised." Merebeth leans over the simmering pot. "It smells good."

Amy tries to shoo her away. "It's a work in progress. Meaning it was supposed to be in progress until you got home." Amy tilts her head. "What are you doing here already? Is everything okay?"

Merebeth takes a deep breath. "Actually, we need to talk about that."

They sit down on the living room sofa. When Merebeth finishes explaining, she feels out of breath. She's not sure she's ever talked so fast, as if even the briefest silence would give Amy too big an opening to object. But when she's finished laying out the details, Amy sits in silence, looking down at her hands. The living room is filled with the mouth-watering aroma of cooking fruit.

"I know it's asking a lot," Merebeth says. She feels like she's said that phrase so many times.

Amy sputters out a breath. "It's already hard being alone so much."

Wendy nods. "I get it."

"Do you?"

"Maybe not."

"I'm glad you can admit that."

"What do you want me to do?"

"You know I can't decide for you."

"But it's not my decision to make on my own. It's ours. I'm changing the game."

"Things always have to change, don't they?" Amy whirls a hand into the air. "The whole world has changed. This doesn't seem so big, I guess."

Merebeth chuckles. "It feels pretty big to me."

Amy reaches over and pulls Merebeth into a hug. She smells of flour and butter and berries. They fall longways onto the sofa, giggling like children. Their faces are close, a strand of Amy's hair in Merebeth's mouth. She doesn't brush it away but lets it linger on her tongue, tasteless. They stare at each other.

"I don't want you to feel abandoned," Merebeth says.

"I never will," Amy says, and the richness of her voice tells Merebeth she means it. "I'm proud of you."

Merebeth torques her head so she can kiss Amy, their lips brushing at an awkward angle. They laugh again. Merebeth sighs and says, "I think it's time to check on your pie. Can I have the first taste?"

Amy sits up and pulls Merebeth with her. Their cheeks are checkered with the imprint of the sofa's fibers. "Is that dirty talk?"

Merebeth smiles. "Maybe?"

"Careful," Amy says. "You're not even in charge of them yet, and you sound like one of your server boys."

SCOTT

GLENN makes the announcement at a meeting on a steamy Saturday at nine in the morning. The entire restaurant staff is crammed in the bump-out, morning sun blaring on a lot of hungover faces. Scott is pretty sure one of the servers hosted a party last night. His invitation must have been lost in the mail. He shrugs it off. He was busy anyway.

Merebeth looks almost embarrassed as Glenn tells them about his leave of absence and her willingness to take over, but that could just be the weirdness of seeing her dressed in a business casual pinstripe suit, her hair styled carefully rather than bunched underneath a colorful bandana. When he asks if anyone has questions no hands go up, but that could be because everyone looks glazed-over, as if they've been dragged out of bed at the crack of dawn, which for college students may as well be the same thing as before noon on a weekend. All the servers are seated at a pair of tables looking seasick, the kitchen staff on the other side of the room looking only marginally less morose. Evan, Scott's normal comrade-in-arms for these meetings, is out of town, so Scott sits alone at a table next to the one occupied by Perry and the bus boys, one of whom keeps jangling his leg up and down. The only person crossing positional lines is Doug, who sits next to Rion, whispering to him periodically.

Scott can see that the cooks have questions. Aside from hiring Rion at the beginning of the summer, the Lake | Drive staff has been miraculously consistent for a long time, and this shakeup is clearly making Wendy, Cynthia, and Satiya uncomfortable. The servers look as if they could not care less. In fact, they'd probably allow for just about any shakeup if it meant some greasy fast food and a nap were coming sooner rather than later.

"What about her replacement?" Wendy asks. "Do you have someone in mind?"

Scott can practically hear it in her voice: pick me.

Glenn nods. "We'll need to do another kitchen hire. So if anyone knows anyone, let me or Merebeth know."

He's so quick to raise his hand he doesn't think about it. Not when Glenn nods toward him does Scott consider what he's doing. Not when he says, "I think I know someone who might be interested."

The night of his lone shift at The Drive, Scott was finishing clearing up the table, having armed himself with a bus tub so no glasses went flying out of the golf cart on the way back, when he heard footsteps. Satiya was long gone, having been able to start her cleanup as soon as the cheesecakes had been served. He looked up, surprised someone would be out at the lake so late.

It was the young woman, Melanie.

Scott stopped scraping out one of the dessert ramekins.

She was standing at the entrance to the gazebo as if waiting for an invitation into a private home. In the glow of the fairy lights, her cheekbones popped. Her eyes were almost watery, but that could have been an effect of the long walk from the restaurant or possibly the impressive amount of alcohol she'd consumed over the course of her meal.

"Hi," she said.

"Hello. Did you forget something?" Scott looked around for a purse or shawl, but the gazebo was bare.

She laughed and shook her head. "No. I just wanted to thank you for the meal. The service was great."

"Thanks."

"I mean it. Prompt, courteous. You know how to wine and dine."

Scott shrugged. "It's pretty easy when you've only got one table."

Melanie laughed and stepped up into the gazebo. She was good-looking, with a heart-shaped face and bright hazel eyes. Her voice was light and, even under the influence of drink, sounded almost like a song, carefully controlled. Scott had never been good at figuring out peoples' ages, but he guessed she was in her mid-twenties, a few years older than him.

"I always wanted to work in a restaurant," she said.

He couldn't decide if she was flirting or not. Had to be, because why else would she be out here?

"It's alright," Scott said. "It pays the rent."

"I guess that's most people's motivation for doing it."

"Not yours?"

She stood directly opposite him at the table, her hands clutching the back of the chair like she was holding on for dear life. Maybe the booze had settled in and she needed it to avoid swaying. "I like talking to people. And I like multi-tasking. I used to watch waitresses all the time. It's like a dance, it seems. An intricate set of steps, trying to be as efficient as possible."

"That's pretty accurate."

"And the kitchen! I used to watch caterers when my parents threw parties. Keeping track of so many requests!" She drummed her fingers on the chair. "I'd love the challenge."

They chatted chummily while Scott finished the last of his cleanup, filling the bus tub with the party's used napkins and silverware. Melanie asked him questions, some he could answer (what was the most annoying drink order for a bartender to make? Were the Thomasville residents good tippers? How often did people dine and dash? Was he always tired?) and some he couldn't (what was the best way to test the doneness of a steak? Which ingredients had the highest overhead? What was in the servesafe solution they used to degrease tables?). If Melanie had somewhere to be or had missed her ride home, she never let on. Scott offered her a ride back to the restaurant when he was finished and she accepted. When he snapped off the fairy lights, cascading the two of them and the gazebo in silvery darkness—the sky was clear, the moon and stars shimmering—she slipped her arm through his.

Scott drove slowly enough that they could have spoken without contesting the breeze, but both he and Melanie were silent on the ride back. He didn't know what to think, or what she wanted. When they climbed into the cart she let go of him, and she spent the entire ride back to Lake | Drive staring out at the water rather than him. But when he came to a halt, she turned to him and thanked him for a nice post-meal experience. Then, as if she'd been holding onto it throughout the entire exchange, maybe the whole meal, she held out a piece of paper: the customer copy of the credit card receipt for dinner, with her phone number written in large, looping handwriting on the back.

"Call me sometime, maybe," she said, hopping from the cart. "Even if it's just to get me a job."

And then, before Scott could say a word, she disappeared around the side of the building, dissolving into the night just as quickly as she had appeared.

They've seen each other twice since then. Scott's heart had choked his throat as he dialed, and he wished she wouldn't answer but she did after three rings, her voice tentative and curious about the mystery of his unfamiliar phone number. As soon as he told her who he was, she went warm and was quick to accept his invitation to one of the coffee shops on the downtown square, a date that lasted long enough to spill into dinner on the downtown square. At the end of the night she kissed him on the cheek and thanked him again, this time for a "real meal." He didn't ask what that meant.

The second time, she surprised him at Lake | Drive, just two days ago while he was working a lunch shift at the bar. He came out of the kitchen with a pair of specials—caprese salads and open-face petit sirloin sandwiches—and saw her perched at the bar. His heart raced as he dropped off the food, and he nearly didn't hear one of the guests ask for an extra side of vinaigrette.

"I hate being surprised," she said by way of greeting, "but I love surprising other people."

"I am surprised," Scott said, setting a coaster in front of her.

"Pleasantly, I hope," she said before ordering a champagne spritzer.

"More than," he said as he mixed it and set it in front of her.

She ordered her own special, then insisted he share the caprese. When he said he wasn't supposed to eat on the clock, she said, "But I'm the customer, and aren't we always right?"

"Industry myth," he said, but plucked up a piece of mozzarella. If she minded that he used his fingers, she didn't say. When she was finished eating, she insisted he call her soon.

So he does, Saturday morning at ten, despite Merebeth and Glenn's suspicions about why the daughter of a university president would want to work in a kitchen. It doesn't matter. Shortly after she answers, voice sleepy, Scott is hanging up, telling his new boss that Melanie will be at the restaurant in under an hour.

CARTER

CARTER suppresses a groan when he checks the time on his phone: four-fifteen. Last time he woke it read two-thirty, and the time before that, one-twenty-six. This has happened every night since Doug's discovery; Carter has put off making a decision about who to awaken and now he's paying the price for that indecision. August has baked the yurt, which doesn't help, either; Carter likes to sleep under at least a sheet, but even doing that adds an extra layer of humidity and warmth that leads to horrible sweating. He's had to shuck the blankets and toss them in the laundry every morning for weeks. It's only a matter of time before his mom says something. His dad won't notice, and Carter's not even sure his father knows where the laundry machines are, much less how to use them or how often doing so is normal.

He doesn't bother trying to get back to sleep; his body is humming with an almost-paranormal energy, the kind of zap that only the dead-tired possess, as if being awake and peppy is an ouroboros loop; if you are sapped enough, you'll suddenly find a second, third, fourth, or, as Carter feels, approximately fortieth, wind. So he sits up, accepting that his day, even if it's still night, is starting.

The good news is that Micha doesn't stir awake. As if possessing an extra sense, he seems to have figured out that Carter's middle-of-the-night excursions are nothing worth waking up for. His breathing stays regular as Carter slithers through the darkness of the yurt. At first, Carter thought Micha was the perfect candidate for receiving his memory, but the more Carter considered it, the less he trusted that instinct. He eventually decided Micha would actually be the worst person in his life to choose: his brother is already wayward, constantly struggling to express himself and find his place in the world; add to that knowing that the world isn't how it ought to be and it would be cruel, rather than kind, for Carter to reformulate his memory. Micha has had a perfectly fine time with the new girl at Temera's Ephemeras, though of course she isn't new to Micha. But what, Carter has thought more than once, would happen if Micha remembered Flower? He can picture the meltdown, the nightmarish aftermath. That is the thing that keeps Carter awake at night.

Who, then, if not his brother? Carter has considered his parents but can come to no conclusions. He tries to imagine what difference it would make to either of them to know the truth, and he comes up with an aching blank. He knows he has to use his ability on someone, at some time. Or does he? When he starts to tumble down these philosophical hedgerows, his head starts to throb.

The night is tar-like with heat and moisture. A cloud of mosquitoes dive-bombs Carter as he exits the yurt. He waves them away even though they never bite; something about his blood type, he read, makes him an unappealing target for feasting, unlike his brother who, after only the briefest stalling outside on summer nights, gets lit up with a constellation of angry bites on his arms and legs.

As he makes his way across the scroll of wet grass, slick tickles collecting at his ankles, Carter is not surprised to see a light on in the kitchen; his mother has also been battling bouts of insomnia. He's overheard Satiya talking about her mother's problems, the late-night phone calls and freak outs. But those are because her mother remembers, which isn't the case here. Carter suspects his mother has been changed by the vanishings, a la Wendy's mom.

"Dude," Donny said, when Carter mentioned the parallel. "You're starting to sound like Doug." Donny has become practically insufferable of late, to the point that Carter has come up with all kinds of excuses not to go home with him, nearly to the point of telling the truth about Micha and his family's local roots. Donny has taken the opposite tack of Doug; where the latter will talk your ear off given the tiniest opening about the disappearances, Donny shuts down. He has seemingly no interest in the fact that the world has completely changed, putting on a front of total disaffection and unconcern. It's rooted, Carter thinks, in Donny's cartoonish libertarianism. The first time Donny said, "Taxation is theft," Carter laughed, thinking he was making a joke. He wasn't.

Carter peeks into the kitchen window from the shadows of the back deck. His mother is leaning over the island with a plate of crackers and cheese. She's deliberate with every movement, as if she's considering each bite she takes. She is facing away from him, so he cannot see the look on her face. He wonders what she's thinking.

To his surprise, his father joins her. Carter can't hear what they're saying, but his father laughs after asking his mother a question, and they sit, side-by-side, turned away from the window. Weirdly, watching them shove sliced cheese and dry saltines into their mouths, even if he can only see the backs of their heads, makes him sleepy, especially when his father puts his arm around his mother's shoulder and pulls her toward him. He wishes, desperately, that he could see their faces and hear their voices. Instead, before they return to bed, he slips off the deck and heads back to the yurt. Micha is still asleep, his wet breathing regular. In the dark, Carter can't see how his brother is arranged on his cot, and he tells himself this is okay. Carter doesn't need to see everything. He slips back under his damp sheet and closes his eyes. To his surprise, when he opens them again, morning has come, Micha already awake, scouring the mini fridge.

They head to Temera's Ephemeras.

The interior of the store is almost as swampy as outside, possibly worse because of the stagnant, unmoving air. As soon as Carter and Micha walk in, the girl, Samantha, apologizes for the sauna-like conditions; the A/C is on the fritz. She's sweltering herself, her spaghetti-strap teal shirt ringed with sweat stains, but she manages to put on a smile for Micha, who seems oblivious to the heat and begins his usual cycle through the wares.

Carter knows next to nothing about Samantha. Unlike Flower, who would talk anyone's ear off—a regular complaint Timothie made, half-heartedly, all the time—Samantha is more reserved, and she and Carter fall into a silence that he can't decide whether to call awkward or comfortable. She never gives him stilted looks or goofy smiles when neither has a thing to say, and she doesn't try to divert attention to Micha while he's absorbed in his product perusal. Carter isn't sure what to say to her or how to ask what her story is, but he is curious about how she came to be at Temera's, or at least what story was created for her if she is a product of the disappearances. But there's never an opening, and Carter isn't creative enough to manufacture one himself.

The restive feeling he got out of seeing his parents has soured in the morning hours, like a gallon of milk left to curdle on a counter. He now feels a stab of anger and jealousy at the affection his father displayed toward his mother. Why not extend that gregariousness to your grown sons, especially the one needing taking care of, a responsibility that has been passed to his brother from his parents? And his mother's restlessness: surely that could be solved by trying to take care of Micha the way she should. Carter can't help but compare their plights and find his own far more justified.

Carter thinks about saying something about it to Samantha, who is busy waving a ratty spiral-bound notebook at her face to keep cool. But again, he can't think of a way in. And then a thought strikes him: what if he gave her her memory back? What would happen if he granted that to one of the replacements? The thought stays with him throughout the remainder of Micha's exploration. It nags and grinds at him. He's pretty sure no one at Lake | Drive has tried it; even though he doesn't keep mental tally of every choice every person has made like Doug does, he's sure he would know if someone had done such a thing. The more he thinks about it, the more intrigued he becomes. He can see himself whiling nights away, considering the possibility. How much more sleep is there to be lost?

Carter and Micha leave empty-handed, as usual. He can't imagine pulling such an experiment in his brother's presence, risking some terrible cataclysm that would further scar Micha. So, he sloughs through a long, terrible shift at work, distracted and disaster-prone, his usual rhythm absent. His tips are terrible. That night, he can't sleep again, so on Saturday he heads, by himself, to Temera's Ephemeras, hoping Samantha will be there.

She is. So are about a dozen mid-morning shoppers, rooting through consigned clothing and discarded toys. Samantha waves and asks where Micha is. He tells her he's sleeping in, which seems to satisfy her curiosity.

He doesn't do it right away. By the time he musters the courage, taking a lap through the store, Samantha is laden with a line of shoppers ready to pay for their scratched records and secondhand jewelry. Carter plucks a beer stein from a shelf with a sticker listing its price at three dollars and gets in the line, which moves surprisingly fast; he is shocked by Samantha's efficiency. When his turn comes, he doesn't let himself hesitate. As Samantha reaches for the stein to check its price, Carter grabs her wrist. Her eyes go wide, and then he says, "I'd like you to remember who you are."

And then, in a blink, Samantha is gone. Standing before him, like she never left, is Flower.

E V A N

IT takes Evan a while to place the girl. He barely gives her any notice when she walks in because she steps up—nearly skipping—to the commercial line, but when Elena says, "Hi, Flower," he looks up so fast he feels a vertebra in his neck make an unpleasant cracking noise.

He only met Flower once, early in his stint at Lake | Drive when he accepted an invitation from Timothie to come over for drinks because he didn't know any better. Despite Timothie's attempts to stuff him with enough cheap red wine to make Evan pliant and horny, all that ended up happening was Evan crashing on the living room couch and being woken way too early in the morning by the sounds of pans being tossed around in the kitchen. He was ready to accost Timothie for making so much noise so early, but Evan, deeply hungover and likely still drunk, instead found himself facing a short, barefoot girl with dirty blonde hair down to her elbows. She had the biggest almond-brown eyes he'd ever seen.

After introducing herself and offering up the briefest of apologies for all the noise, Flower launched into her life story, told so fast that Evan›s addled brain could hardly keep up. Something about rich asshole parents whose major sin he couldn›t quite sort out and loving Timothie but not like that and was Evan a friend from work or school or both and did he want some eggs, which she cooked every weekend morning to help alleviate Timothie's headaches.

He did stay for the eggs. Flower became quiet and considerate as he ate, staring at him with hopeful expectation. He nodded and she smiled. The eggs were good, salty and creamy, the yolks rich and thick. They didn't make his hangover disappear, but they did settle his stomach enough that he could drive home.

Evan watches her interaction with Elena. He knows she works at Temera›s Ephemeras on the square, and that for a long time she used her lunch break on Fridays to make a quick deposit at the bank, often enough a combination of business funds as well as her bi-weekly paycheck. So the fact that she and Elena are chummy is no surprise.

What surprises Evan is her presence, because as far as he knows, she is one of the ones who disappeared.

He slips into the bowels of the bank during a lull, glancing into the manager›s office; Denise is there, hunched over one of the many stacks of paperwork cluttering her desk. Evan feels a brief sorrow. He thought maybe everything had clicked back into place, that those who had vanished had returned and he would find Salazar in his rightful spot. Denise has been okay, treating Evan neither poorly nor well. She doesn't seem to notice him at all.

Evan spends the afternoon wondering about Flower and what her presence means, how it happened. As he drives to the restaurant, he wonders about the disappearances, squirming for a reason. Something so big, so world-tilting and rearranging has to have some meaning, some purpose. As with his own meandering, wandering life, they seem to have no coherent purpose, no driving rationale.

When he steps out of his car at Lake | Drive, he hears someone call his name. Carter, clutching his apron, jogs from his car to meet Evan.

"You won›t believe what I did," Carter says. His face is bright red. "With my one person I can make remember, I mean."

Evan thinks he has some idea.

Doug just about loses his mind when he finds out, which makes Evan smile. He likes Doug even though everyone likes to rag on him except Rion. Timothie and Donny make comments about the two and their hookups, but Evan is observant enough to know when something is more than just sex and lusty attraction. Amidst all the summer chaos, the fact that Doug and Rion have found each other is particularly impressive to Evan.

In fact, Rion seems to have tempered Doug›s spastic tendencies following the disappearances, but even his calming influence is nothing when Doug hears about the reappearance of Flower. Evan shrugs when Doug's interrogation turns his way, and he listens while Carter and Timothie are subjected to endless questioning that doesn›t really go anywhere. The kitchen ladies look on with what to Evan seems to be mixed interest: Merebeth is too busy being the boss to really absorb the newest twist, and Satiya has a defeated look on her face. Wendy glares hard from the line. When Angela comes into the kitchen she listens carefully, her investment caught by no one else, it seems, except maybe Rion, who stares at her with a tilted head and squinting eyes. The new girl, Melanie, just looks confused. Evan hasn›t interacted with her much except when she›s finished her shifts and has, unlike the other women of the kitchen, broken through the membrane separating front of house from back and sidled up to the bar, ordering a glass of champagne and waiting for Scott to show up. Melanie didn›t retroactively receive her memories by virtue of being hired; she›s been just as clueless as all the outsiders.

Until today, at least, when, during the Flower hullabaloo, Donny, of all people, seeing her bewilderment, walks up to her, wraps a hand around her bicep, and says, "Allow me. Please remember."

DONNY

DONNY'S thinking, mostly, is fuck it. He's not given anyone their memory back, and the new chick—total smoke show, but clearly has her eye set on that asshole Scott—is as good a choice as any. Who else is he going to pick? His douchebag dad who thinks being a good father is sending a five-dollar bill and nothing else in an envelope every year on Donny's birthday? An envelope clearly designed to hold a card? Like the kind you only really come to possess when you have bought a card, and thus have made the overt decision not to send said card but instead only the measly fuck-you five bucks? Or his mom, who seems to have forgotten he exists, never returning his phone calls unless he calls her three times in the same day? The mom who always sounds delirious, as though Annette has been selling to her, too? The mom who doesn't ever remember any of her promises, which is no surprise considering she was always forgetting about doctor's appointments and soccer practice? He's lucky he didn't have child leukemia or something, and it's probably her fault he's not the next Pele.

So, fuck it. Melanie it is.

How, he wonders afterward, can it possibly be his fault she collapses?

Like, has Doug mentioned this side effect? Has anyone given any warning this might happen? Donny's pretty god damn sure the answer is no.

And yet, as soon as Melanie falls to the floor, the rubber non-skid mats making her landing gentle enough that no one should worry about any fractured bones, everyone is screaming at him. Wendy is shrieking nonsense like he has assaulted the girl, and Carter is saying, "What the fuck?" over and over. Doug is shaking his head. Merebeth screams for everyone to give her and Melanie some room. Angela, of all people, looks weirdly serene. Fortunately, Scott isn't around, or surely he'd be looking to cut off Donny's balls or some shit.

Melanie is quick to recover, coming out of her stupor as Merebeth kneels down and places a hand on her forehead as if she's expecting Melanie to be feverish, like Donny has passed on some fast-acting influenza instead of altered her memories. Evan appears, ever gallant, with a glass of water. She takes it with a quivering hand and drinks a long gulp, then looks around the kitchen, first at Merebeth and then the assemblage that is crowded on the line, her eyes landing eventually on Donny.

"What did you do to me?"

"That depends on what you remember," he says.

"Who is the president?" Doug says.

She squints in thoughtful concentration, and for a second Donny thinks he›s actually fucked up, that her memory of the world has been totally wiped out. But then she says the first asshole's name and then corrects herself, or at least stops, confused by her own knowledge, and says the first one again.

"She›s okay," Donny says. "It worked, see?"

No one is listening to him, too busy treating Melanie like a delicate baby bird even though it's obvious she›ll be just fine. Eventually, after she finishes the water, she stands up with Merebeth's help. The kitchen ladies suggest she take a few minutes, and Merebeth opens up the office, where she orders Melanie to take a seat. Everyone is glaring at Donny, so he shoves out of the kitchen to check on his one table.

Later, Merebeth asks Donny to wait on a twenty-five top that comes in at six-thirty. He knows she chooses him not for his sunny personality and serving abilities but because he's the only option: Timothie is swamped in the bump-out, Carter has been summoned to The Drive, and the other servers are in the largest, fullest sections. Even Angela is frazzled. Donny, however, has a simple two-booth, two-table section that is currently home to a quartet of couples who have their food. So he says sure.

The group is a bunch of kiddie baseball players and their parents from out of town. If their initial glimpses of the menu are any indication, they didn›t realize the price range and upscale nature of their chosen eatery until after they've arranged themselves in the back party room. The kiddos are still in their uniforms, half of them streaked with dirt and grass stains. The dads wear khaki shorts and sweat-stained t-shirts, unlike their peers in the dining room in sports coats and wing tips. The moms appear the most embarrassed thanks to their jean shorts and tank tops.

Everyone splits up by demographics rather than family. Donny›s ready for this skull fuckery, though, and asks the parentals to tell him their kids' jersey numbers every time they order something. The moms fawn over this system, the dads guffawing as if Donny has discovered the secret of the fucking universe or the cure for cancer. He waits until he›s standing at the bar, watching Evan pile bottles of Bud Light onto a tray—Donny nearly laughed out loud when one of the men asked if Lake | Drive did buckets or pitchers—to roll his eyes.

Even if the kids are annoying and the parents drunk halfway through the meal thanks to a day of sun and driving, Donny has to admit, as he's splitting up their checks, that he's grateful for the hustle and bustle; it has given him no time to think about the Melanie business and has kept him from the chatter about Flower, who he barely knew but didn›t think much of. She reeked of hipster rich girl rejecting her wealthy roots simply because she could, as if she would become a better person by casting off her bank account for the sake of what she›d call simple living, a move Donny finds ridiculously stupid and also insulting to people who have to actually work hard.

The party compliments him on getting all of their bills exactly right, though Donny can tell these cheapskates don't usually sup in places that charge five dollars for a bottle of domestic beer. They reek of shitty tipping, and his expectations are low, so he's pleasantly surprised when he gathers up the credit card slips and discovers that he's been given over twenty percent by every family. The people of Thomasville and the surrounding area, in Donny's experience, are usually stingy, viewing tipping as a burden that is sometimes not a necessity. The staff have an ever-expanding list of guests who, no matter the quality of service, never grat more than ten percent.

As he's clearing all the plates and glasses from the table, tossing the last of a heap of crumpled napkins from the kids' table into a bus tub, he hears the louvered doors separating the back room from the dining room open. Donny turns and sees Carter, who has taken half of his section while he's been waiting on the baseball team. He slouches down in an empty seat and flicks a finger at a sweaty glass still half full of Sprite.

"You look like shit," Donny says.

Carter shakes his head. "Haven›t been sleeping."

Donny raises an eyebrow. It›s been a few weeks since the two have hooked up. Donny assumed Carter has found someone else or something.

"This Flower thing has me all messed up." Carter slumps forward and folds his arms on the table, resting his head atop the tangle of limbs. "Like, what did I do?"

Donny sits down next to him. He›s not sure what to say. Flirting and sex are one thing; those he finds easy. But he can tell Carter is actually upset. Donny lays a hand on his back, can feel the vertebrae of Carter›s spine rearing up like an architectural wonder between his muscles.

"You kind of saved her, bro."

"Saved her from what?"

"I dunno. Nonexistence? Annihilation? I›m not the philosophy major."

Carter lets out a fake laugh. "I don›t think Andre taking one class makes him a philosopher."

"Why do you feel messed up?"

Carter›s head rocks back and forth, forehead pivoting on one of his wrists. "I don›t know. I feel sick. Like someone gave me the flu."

"Well, I sure don't have Chlamydia."

"You sure know how to make people feel better."

Donny pats Carter on the back. "I sure do." He waggles his eyebrows and Carter lets out a laugh, real this time.

The sound of Carter laughing does something weird to Donny, and before he knows what's happening, he's leaning over and brushing his lips in a gentle peck along the side of Carter's throat. They've kissed before, obviously, done way, way more than that, but never has something like this passed between them, a gesture of intimacy and, fuck, maybe compassion. Carter sits up straight and turns to look at Donny, who is still leaning close.

"When we get out of here," Carter says, "can I show you something?"

"Sure dude. Whatever." He shrugs, but his heart is pounding.

Carter leaves. Donny finishes cleaning up the private room, draping the tables with fresh linens and silverware sets even though there's no party on the books for the rest of the weekend. He runs the Bissell over the carpet, where straw wrappers, bits of gristle, breadcrumbs, and the torn-up label of a Bud bottle have been strewn by nervous hands. By the time he's finished the dinner rush is effectively over, his section empty. Merebeth cuts the floor. Donny rolls his helping of silverware, where he's joined by Andre and Andrew, then finally Carter, who makes no mention of whatever it is he wants to show Donny. Not until Donny clocks out and waits for Carter to emerge from the office after doing his cash out, pocketing that night's scroll of bills, does either acknowledge the request.

Carter pulls his car keys from his pocket. "Ready?"

"You›re driving?"

"It›ll be easier."

"Why?"

"Can I please just show you before I change my mind?"

"Shit," Donny says. "Okay. Sure."

They climb into Carter's car, the chill of the air conditioning a blessing against the swarthy night. Mosquitoes dive bomb the headlights and the Lake | Drive marquee. For the first few minutes of the drive the car is silent. Donny thinks about saying something stupid or silly, but he recognizes that this is a moment to shut the fuck up. Finally, as they enter Thomasville and Carter turns into a neighborhood that Donny's never stepped foot in, Carter speaks.

"You›ve probably wondered why we›ve only ever gone to your place." Then, before Donny can say yes, he has wondered but hasn›t really cared because who cares where you're hooking up with someone, Carter adds, "And you might also be wondering why I tried to make that girl at Temera's remember. You might be wondering what I was doing there in the first place."

Donny wants to say that no, he hasn›t thought much about either of those things. He hasn't wondered, because until now he hasn't cared very much about the disappearances and the resilience of his memory and that of the others at Lake | Drive. He hasn't been awed by their ability to give memory back. Hence: Melanie. But there's something aching and yearning in Carter's voice, something that sets the back of Donny's neck tingling.

Fuck, Donny thinks. I think I'm falling in god damn fucking love.

Carter pulls into the driveway of a ranch-style house. An American flag, affixed against a white column, whips in the night wind. They climb out of the car, but instead of heading to the door, Carter leads them around the side of the house. The last fireflies dot the yard with their ethereal light, zipping away as Donny and Carter pass.

They approach a yurt at the far reaches of the long, scrolling yard. Questions ache to burst from Donny's lips but he swallows them down in what he feels is the greatest show of willpower of his life. They stop at a canvas flap and Carter turns to him.

"I›ve never shown anyone this before." His voice is wobbly and Donny wishes he could see Carter's face clearly but the inky night is uncooperative. Carter clears his throat. "And if I show you, you have to promise not to be an asshole. Can you do that?"

Donny feels a sour warmth rise in his throat. Dizziness surrounds the edges of his vision. He isn't sure what is happening or what he's about to see, but the urge to say yes overpowers him. He nods and says sure, okay. Of course. Yes.

"Alright," Carter says, lifting the canvas. Eggy light spills out of the yurt. "I want you to meet my brother, Micha."

A N D R E W

THE state highway leading to St. Matthew's is all scutch grass and crepe myrtles that rustle with the afternoon breeze. The only color besides the bright blasts of green and wheat are the occasional spray of buttercups and the chocolate darkness of fresh-tilled soil. After so many trips to the home, Andrew isn't worried that he will accidentally careen into a ditch or a tree if he pays more attention to the passing landscape than the road itself; his body has memorized its dips and curves. Like any other place where human beings shunt off examples of genetics at its failing worst, St. Matthew's is tucked away in the middle of nowhere, three miles outside a town so tiny it makes Thomasville look like a booming metropolis.

"Thanks for coming," he says.

"No problem," Andre says.

It took Andrew a long time to tell Andre the truth about Jessica. He's the first person to know besides his immediate family; some cousins are still further in the dark than Andre is. After the disappearances, he just blurted it out one night after work. They were sitting in Andrew's living room, the tiny space illuminated by an LED candle and the porch light than bled through the blinds. They were drinking Blue Moons and decompressing. Hadn't taken their clothes off or kissed or anything. The overwhelming confusion of the changed world had left Andrew feeling raw. And so he just let everything spill out. Andre leaned back in surprise at first, more, he would say later, at the rapid-fire, voluminous spillage coming out of Andrew's mouth than their actual content. When Andrew was finished, Andre took a sip of his beer, which had been sweating in his hand the entire time, and said, "Do you see her much?"

The answer is yes. St. Matthew's is halfway between Hannibal and St. Louis on highway 61, curled away from civilization on a long swath of land buttressed by nothing but fields. Andrew and his parents visited her every month during Andrew's final year of high school, and he'd made a few trips down during his freshman year, promising himself he would keep going. But of course he didn't, the visits become more and more infrequent each semester. Andrew has told himself that this is how life is: that school work and having a life cause redirections of the current, that it is only natural that he has slowly drifted away from Jessica and even his mom and dad. But the reality, he knows—and this he also admitted to Andre after a long exhalation of beery breath—is that he's worried he'll be struck, too. That, somehow, if he stays away from Jessica he won't suffer her fate, as if her illness is contagious.

"I know it's stupid," he said.

Andre, shaking his head, laid a hand on Andrew's thigh. "No, it isn't." Then he offered to come with Andrew. Not for moral support, necessarily, but in case Andrew wanted someone else besides Jessica to remember. "Like her doctor."

Andrew felt a sudden heat in his jaw. He hadn't told Andre that he planned to give Jessica her memory back; Andre simply knew. Andrew, in turn, simply nodded, and now here they are, passing through the dust-strewn town whose only attractions are a two-pump gas station and attendant convenience mart plus auto repair facility on one side of the street and a shadowy bar whose opaque windows give off the vibe of a seedy strip club on the other. They pass through the only intersection—a two-way stop, so they don't even have to slow down—and are out of the tiny enclave before they've had time to process it.

If Andre is surprised by the appearance of St. Matthew's—its curved drive and brick facade burst from the trees and fields like a sudden, unexpected obelisk—he doesn't show it. He says nothing of the wrought-iron gate and fencing, or about the fact that the building, with its cream-colored concrete edging, looks like it belongs more on the McClain campus than stuck in the middle of nowhere. Andre is silent as Andrew pulls up to an intercom box and gives their names and Jessica's. He says not a word as the gate clanks open and they drive around the side of the long three-story building and pull into a parking spot.

"You're sure about this?" Andrew says.

"If I said no would we leave?" Andre asks, but he's smiling, which makes Andrew smile, too.

They walk through a side entrance. A woman takes their driver's licenses, even though she must have dozens, hundreds, of copies of Andrew's. When she returns them, she also hands them bright orange visitor badges they are instructed not to take off for any reason. She is one of at least three replacements that Andrew has observed at St. Matthew's. The old intake nurse, a woman in her fifties named Esther, always remembered Andrew and his parents, treated them with excessive kindness, speaking well of Jessica even if there was really nothing good to say. This new woman, a brunette in her twenties who will not look either Andrew or Andre in the eye, gives brusque instructions on where Jessica's wing is, even though Andrew already knows. She calls an orderly to lead them to the day room.

Andrew watches Andre take in the blank beige walls, the eerie quiet, the random resident mumbling to himself. The closed doors of private rooms, the ignored ping pong table folded up in a hallway. They pass through a pair of heavy doors that open only when the orderly swipes a badge against a card reader. Andrew feels the back of his neck tingle even though Andre's face is placid.

When Andrew told Andre the truth about his sister, he wanted Andre to ask more questions. Like, was Andrew worried that one day he would start seeing things, hearing things, inhabiting a world occupied by no one but himself? Because he is, every day, convinced that he will suffer like Jessica. The day of the disappearances he had been terrified, convinced his bill of bad health had finally come due. But of course it hadn't, unless the entire world was going crazy along with him.

Jessica is sitting in a green wing-back chair, the dark plush of its crushed velvet amplifying the alabaster color of her skin. Andrew feels like he and his sister look nothing alike thanks to his golden glow from spending his afternoons at the apartment complex pool. Jessica has gained weight from the nutritionally thoughtless institutional food, whereas Andrew, thanks to his boyish metabolism and summer regiment of jogging and pushups, is trim and fit. The recognition of their difference makes him ache. He grits his teeth.

His sister doesn't notice him or Andre until they get close. She's staring out a wide, pristine window—recently cleaned; he can see the streaks, glowy with the slightest prism of rainbow colors—toward a field behind the building, unkempt stalks of grass and wheat. A notebook is perched on one of the chair's arms, turned to a clean page. Jessica holds a pen, the tip pressed to the paper. Andrew sees that there's nothing written there.

"Hey, sis," he says when he gets close.

She turns slowly to face him, as if she is a machine in need of oiling. When she's looking straight at him, she smiles. Andrew is happy to see her teeth are clean and white as always.

"Hi Drewie." Her nickname for him. The only person he ever let call him that, their parents included.

"Drewie," Andre says.

"Hi Jessie." Andrew points at Andre, who gives a little wave. "This is my friend Andre."

She gives him a knowing wink. "A friend?"

Andre laughs. "Something like that."

"Drewie's never brought a friend with him before."

"I guess I'm lucky. It's nice to meet you."

"You love my brother enough to come all this way?"

Andrew feels flush, but Andre laughs, tilts his head back, elongating his neck, the elegant muscles of his throat sliding and pulsing. "Something like that."

"I'm happy to hear that." She turns her gaze to Andrew. "This makes me happy, Drewie."

"I'm glad," Andrew says.

Jessica turns her attention back to the window and the scroll of weeds and chaff behind the building. Andrew follows her gaze; whether she sees anything more than he does, he has no way of knowing. Andre is shifting his weight from one leg to another, his hands stuffed in his jeans pockets. When Andrew glances at him, Andre smiles. His teeth beam white.

"Have you been writing?" Andrew asks. When they were younger, Jessica wanted to be a writer. Every Christmas and birthday she would ask for a new Moleskine because she'd filled her last one with poems and character sketches and stories and diary entries. One of the worst moments of her breakdown occurred when one of her doctors wanted to read through her journals to see if he could glean anything about what had happened. Their parents agreed. Jessica did not. Andrew understood that they were trying to help, desperate to do whatever it took to make Jessica better. But these were her private thoughts and ideas, creative output she protected like children of her own. She screamed and balked and even tried to run away with as many of the Moleskines as she could carry, but she didn't get far, the leather books slipping and sliding against one another and rattling out of her arms in a flurry of limned paper that scattered on the sidewalk.

She turns to look at Andrew. "A little. Here and there."

"What do you write about?" Andre asks.

Her eyes go moony. "About the world. About the people in it."

"Like who?"

"People who are a mystery to me."

Andrew sucks in a breath. Since coming to St. Matthew's two years ago, Jessica has made no mention of the men, but he knows that's who she's talking about. He glances at Andre, silently willing him to change the subject.

"So, everyone?" Andre says. "I find everyone mysterious."

"All the world's a mystery," Jessica says.

"Shakespeare?"

Jessica laughs. It sounds like glass breaking. "He called it a play."

Andre shrugs. "Same thing, as far as I›m concerned. Right?" He looks at Andrew.

"My brother isn›t very philosophical."

"I›m not sure that›s true."

"I am."

"I guess that settles that."

No one speaks. Andrew feels sick. He mumbles something about going to the bathroom. He crosses the day room, feeling Jessica's eyes on him. Andre stares at him with one eyebrow raised. Andrew gives a little shake of his head.

The washroom is tiny, the mirror covered in a sheet of unbreakable plastic. The toilet has no lid, and the paper is scratchy. Andrew splashes cold water on his face and looks at himself in the mirror. He feels an odd mix of sorrow and shame. The former he always feels in some measure when he sees his sister, but the latter is confounding. Perhaps because he had it in his head he could somehow fix her? Maybe even that he considered the notion that she needs fixing in the first place. But that's ridiculous. Of course she does. But would realigning her memory be a fix at all? He doubts his decision to give Jessica her memory back. She seems content. Her eyes are soft and warm, her face devoid its usual tension. Perhaps the disappearances have swept away the worst of her demons.

When he emerges from the bathroom, Jessica is scribbling in her notebook. Andre stands off to the side of her chair looking out the window. The tableau is nice, Andrew thinks, and he watches for a while, his return unnoticed. The day room is quiet. Most of the patients are like his sister, prone to quiet contemplation rather than irrational outbursts. When he asked her after she first moved in what the other residents were like, she paused for a moment and said, "Thoughtful."

After a while, he makes his presence known, clapping Andre on the shoulder. "How are we doing?" he says.

Andre turns. "Your sister is writing me a poem."

"That's nice. What's it about?"

"You'd have to ask her."

They both look at Jessica, who pays them no mind. She is writing fast in small, compact cursive that resembles the dribbling line of a seismograph. Jessica's teachers used to constantly complain about her handwriting, but Andrew took pride in never having any trouble deciphering what it said. It was as if he was the only one who could understand what she was saying.

Andrew and Andre sit on a nearby sofa and watch Jessica write. She's at it for a long time, and Andrew is grateful that Andre makes no effort to fill the silence. He doesn't yank out his phone and start texting or surfing social media. What he does do is take Andrew's hand in his and lay both of them on his thigh, his fingers holding Andrew's tight.

TIMOTHIE

SHE came bursting into the apartment one Friday, thirty minutes before Timothie left for his work shift. He wasn't surprised to see her, exactly, because he'd come home from brunch and found that all of Flower's things were back where they belonged. And when she came whirling in, she was exactly her same self, talkative, voice a babbling brook that made no attempt to explain her long absence.

And that›s the funny thing: Flower doesn't seem to realize she was ever gone. When she flapped into the apartment, he asked her, experimentally, what she'd done the weekend before and she laughed, slapped his arm, and said that she remembered getting hammered on champagne with him, how they'd tried and failed to make homemade donuts at two in the morning. She held up her arm, even, and showed off a still-pink burn across her forearm. The sight made Timothie dizzy, not because he was squeamish about scar tissue but because the idea that someone remembered him doing something that he clearly hadn't—or at least that he didn't remember, a can of worms he didn't want to even pick up—made him feel like he was on the bucking bow of a ship.

"I guess it makes sense," Doug says. They're standing at the salad station, Timothie ignoring the fact that he needs to set four tables in the bump-out in the next ten minutes. Doug is prepping artichoke hearts and washing heads of iceberg lettuce. At first, Doug gave Timothie the side-eye, which he guesses is fair: they never talk. But Timothie was—

is—desperate, and he hates to admit it, but no one else has their head wrapped around this whole thing better than Doug.

"It does?"

"Well, as much as any of it can make sense."

Doug is nice enough, Timothie supposes. Not bad to look at, either, if a bit short. Clearly works out, if the way his biceps press out from the sleeves of his t-shirts is any indication. There's just something about him, being in the salad station rather than out on the floor. Plus, he's obsessive over all this disappearances nonsense.

"She'd need to have something in her head from all that time away," Doug says.

"Away?"

Doug blinks. "I'm not sure what else to call it. She's probably the only person on the planet who was gone and is here again. Unless someone else used their one shot the way Carter did."

"So that's it?"

"There's not, like, an instruction manual or anything. What else do you want me to say?"

"Fine. Jeez." Timothie escapes into the dining room. Evan is busy drying martini glasses at the bar while Merebeth scribbles something in a ledger at one of the barstools, a condensing glass of water before her. It's still strange to see her in sheer peach-colored blouses and slacks, with flats on instead of Crocs, though they're certainly a fashionable improvement. And who knew she has decent hair when she sets it free from those hideous bandanas the line cooks are always wearing? Timothie understands health code protocols, but still. Merebeth is actually pretty decent looking when she's cleaned up. He guesses that's the difference between people: some look good no matter what. Others take more work.

He plucks tablecloths from the stack beneath the back server station and hauls them into the bump-out. Not only is Timothie glad he's always working these reservations with their set menus because of the inherently excellent gratuities that come along with them, he's also always liked the serenity of the bump-out; it's like a Florida room, separate from the busy humdrum of the dining room. Even though there's no actual wall segregating it from the rest of the restaurant, some invisible aura manages to change the mood when he's in the bump-out. He can forget about the bustle of the restaurant for a while, the echo of the three walls of windows creating something serene and near-silent; diners in the bump-out, which only contains half a dozen tables, seem to somehow know to keep their voices low. They drink their pricey wines and enjoy their amuse-bouche and niçoise without loud guffaws of laughter or the heavy clink of silverware being dropped to the porcelain of plates.

Timothie has his back turned to the restaurant interior, but he hears footsteps where the floor switches from terra cotta ceramic to high-quality wood vinyl. He turns: Merebeth is watching him, hands in the pockets of her wool slacks.

"I was wondering," she says.

Timothie frowns. "Yeah?"

"Would you mind if we let Rion serve two of the reservations in here tonight?"

"Rion? Why?"

Merebeth shrugs. "I think it would be good for someone else to have some practice."

"But I always do the bump-out."

"I know that. That's what I'm saying. We should have someone else who knows how."

"But why?"

"You don't think it would be a good idea for some other people to have some experience?"

"What else would I do all night?"

"You two can split a section in the dining room. He's got four tables, so you'd each have two of those and two of these."

"Seems complicated."

"Well, I could just have him do the whole bump-out, but I didn't think you'd like that idea."

Timothie can feel his face going red. "You're right about that."

"So doesn't half-and-half seem like a good compromise?"

Timothie's been holding a bunch of forks in his left hand, like he's clutching a metallic bouquet. He's tempted to toss them on the floor. Instead, he sets them down on the nearest table in a snarl of tines. "Have I done something wrong?"

"Of course not."

"Because this feels like punishment for something."

"Listen, Tim," she says. Timothie grits his teeth; he hates being called Tim. It isn't his name. But he says nothing. "How long have you worked here?"

"Since I was eighteen." He'd seen a call for servers on the bulletin board in his dorm; someone had managed to shove it in among the posters for fraternity and sorority rush events, the eight-thousand on-campus clubs, the advertisements for tutoring services. Timothie didn't really need a job, but he'd found himself bored by his first semester's classes, all general education garbage that felt like high school all over again, classes he was taking because he didn't yet know what he wanted to do with the rest of his life. So, he'd plucked down the flyer whole-sale even though it was one of those with tearable strips at the bottom.

When he called the number and then showed up for the interview on a Monday at three in the afternoon, when he should have been in his psychology lecture, he'd walked out with the job and a first shift that coming Wednesday.

"So over three years," Merebeth says. "And you're the only one who ever works the bump-out. You don't think that's a problem?"

"Only if the way I work it is a problem."

Merebeth sighs and raises her hands in supplication. "Of course it's not. It's just." She looks around the room, out the windows and toward the lake, which is peaceful and cerulean, afternoon light twinkling off the surface. "You don't want to work here the rest of your life, do you?"

"I don't know," Timothie says. He looks down at his feet, then at hers. "Do you?"

"Do I what?"

"Want to work here the rest of your life?"

She crosses her arms. "I don't know. Honestly. It's a good job, a good place to be. But you can go anywhere."

"How do you know?"

She steps closer. "Because I know you, Tim."

He shakes his head but then says, "Fine. Sure. Do whatever you want with the bump-out." He picks up the silverware. "Have Rion come in here. I'll show him how to set up."

She sets a hand on his shoulder. It is meaty and heavy. "Thanks. I appreciate it."

"Of course," he says, forcing a smile. "Any time."

The evening runs smoothly enough, though Timothie feels a begrudging annoyance every time a table is sat in the dining room in his and Rion's shared section and it's his turn to take it. He watches Rion nimbly manage the prix fixe menu, rattling off the five courses to his two tables: Peruvian yellow potatoes with Amarillo peppers and Botija olives; grilled sea scallops; a filet mignon seco; a hand-selected cheese board; and Satiya's famed crème brulee to finish things off. Rion's guests nod, order their wine, enjoy each plate, laugh at his pithy comments as he clears dishes. At the tail end of the evening, as Timothie is printing the bill for one of his regular tables, he says, "How's it going?" as Rion stands by the bar, waiting for a glass of Antigal Uno to deliver to his own last dining room table.

"Just fine. Easier than I thought."

"It's nice, when they only have to think about what they want to drink."

Rion nods. "Takes some of the guesswork out."

"It's true."

"Thanks for letting me do it."

"It wasn't really a choice."

"Well," Rion says as Evan sets down the wine glass in front of him, Rion spearing the wet ticket onto the stack of completed bar orders, "in that case, I at least appreciate you not trying to sabotage me."

Merebeth emerges from the kitchen, where the sizzle of meat and clatter of plates has subsided; the Hobart's rumble as Cynthia runs another rack of drinking glasses and soup bowls is noticeable. The dining room has cooled off, the dinner rush slowing down to a trickle, so Merebeth announces that she's cutting the floor. Just as Timothie pockets the bill for his table into a check book, she says, "Do you mind if Rion stays on as long instead of you?"

Timothie looks from her to him, Rion suddenly appearing sheepish. Angela comes barreling around the corner, arms laden with dirtied plates, and nearly crashes into him. He feels Merebeth watching him as he delivers the check to his table, the man in a too-large Joseph A.

Bank suit jacket already prepared with a shimmering silver Amex card. When Timothie returns to the station to run it, he says, not looking at either Rion or Merebeth, "Now it feels like I'm being given the boot."

She sighs. "It's just like what I said earlier. Do you want to be the long server every night? For the rest of your life?"

"Maybe not the rest of my life," Timothie says, yanking the credit card slip as it prints out. He stuffs it in the check presenter. "But for tonight, yes. This is my life. And you're taking it."

He walks off before she can respond.

His table in the bump-out is gone, so Timothie plucks up the credit card slip—a pleasant surprise of an extra fifteen dollars on top of the automatic gratuity—and clears the table. Then he starts breaking everything down, pulling the tablecloths from both his and Rion's tables, stacking the last dirtied dessert dishes and spoons crusty with bruleed egg yolk. He sweeps out the room, tosses the dirtied linens in the laundry basket near the dish station. Then he gets to work on the back station side work, combining two half-full tea urns into one and taking the other to the dish pit, where Cynthia slides out of his way so he can rinse it out. He asks her to run the silverware, and she nods. He removes two of the water pitchers from their saucers and dumps their contents into the sink while Cynthia runs the knives and forks. He marries steak sauces and wipes out bottles of Grey Poupon. When the silverware is ready to be rolled, he takes the rack into the back room, which is where Rion finds him.

"You didn›t have to do all that," Rion says.

"Just trying to help out. It›s what people usually do for the long server."

Rion sits down across from him. Carter pokes his head in and says he›ll be in to help as soon as he dishes out portions of sour cream for the expo line.

"I didn›t ask her to do any of this, you know," Rion says.

"I know."

"Then why are you giving me the cold shoulder?"

"I›m not."

"Sure feels like it." When Timothie says nothing, Rion says, "It's not like I want to spend all night here."

"Big plans with Doug?"

Rion sighs. "You know, Merebeth was right. You don›t want to spend your whole life here, do you?"

"Where else would I go?" Timothie sets down a set of rolled silver in his pile. "And with who?"

Rion lets out a scratch of noise: a laugh or a scoff. Timothie can›t tell which. "Dude, haven›t you 'gone' with just about everyone who works here?"

"Well, those wells have pretty much dried up, haven't they?"

Rion frowns. "I guess."

"And that's not what I mean."

"Then what do you mean?"

Timothie leans back, the forelegs of his chair lifting off the floor. He crosses his arms. "I don't know. Just, it's seeing you and Doug and all the others finding each other. There's not much left for me. Besides my work here."

"This isn't all there is," Rion says.

"Sure feels like it." Timothie looks past him toward the dining room, empty except for a few tables in Angela's section. "I've spent three summers now doing nothing but working here. And what do I have to show for it but having someone else horn in on my territory?" He holds up a hand before Rion can object. "I know, you're not. I'm being dramatic. Let me have it, okay?"

"Okay."

"It's just, like, shouldn't there be more? By now?"

"Maybe there is and you just don>t know it."

"Well, I'd sure like to know it sooner than later."

Carter, as promised, comes in through the kitchen door. Before he reaches them, Rion leans forward and says, "Well, here's something: I think I know who caused the disappearances."

PART FIVE

Y O U

SOMEONE *knows.*

You should care, but you do not.

In fact, you're glad, in a way. It is lonely being the only one. And you've seen how loneliness can be erased, transfigured, replaced. You are warmed by the knowledge that you do not carry this thing that you created alone anymore. You're ready to speak it, to sing it, to share it.

R I O N

HE'S been mulling it all for a while now.

Hearing Doug has helped, though often enough his theories are a babbling brook, noise to fill up the time when they lie next to each other, bodies tingling, a fan on Rion's desk blowing cool air over them. He's not always listening, but he always nods.

No, what has really helped has been watching.

Every time Doug has made a discovery, Rion has watched. When Doug noticed that they all remembered and no one else did, Rion observed his fellow employees. Their body language, their faces. When Doug told them about his roommate's memory, Rion watched. The quick jolts of shock, the expressive, involuntary twitches of muscle. The ways a façade would break without intent. And then the crash that Melanie took: he watched the way Satiya and Wendy and Cynthia were aghast, quick to rush to her aid. How, at the revelation about Flower, every one of the wait staff betrayed at least the slightest surprise, even if, like Donny, they were trying to tamp it down.

All but one of them.

He waits until Merebeth has told him to start on his side work, wiped his name off the laminated floor chart at the hostess stand. He waits until he's finished clearing his tables and vacuuming beneath chair legs, stocking pint glasses at the soda gun, refilling the ice bin. Evan is talking to a pair of guests at the far end of the bar, where they perch on their stools and drink martinis, the woman licking her fingers to get the last vestiges of spice from the dusted Cajun shrimp cocktail she and her date have scarfed down. Carter and Donny are sitting a few seats down, sipping beers. Timothie, who took in Rion's theory without a word of reaction, is already gone, marched out into the night with his apron in his fist with barely a goodbye to anyone, as if he's been demoted or, worse, fired. But Rion knows he'll be back.

He waits in the back room, a fresh set of silverware steaming on one of the tables. Doug, finally finished cleaning up the salad station, joins him.

"You're sure about this?"

"No," Rion says. "But close enough."

Eventually, he thinks, she'll show up.

And eventually, she does.

Angela.

She's done something to her hair, which has always been blonde but is now lighter, a flaxen platinum that shimmers with the slightest touch of gold as if light itself has been woven into the strands. Even in the low glow of the private dining room it shines as if spotlit. Rion watches Angela look around, as if she isn't seeing him even though he's seated in the very center of the space. When her eyes alight on them she seems to relax, as though not being able to track his presence has created a gnawing disturbance in her gut. He says nothing as she trots over and pulls out the chair opposite him and sits down, exactly where Timothie sat not long ago.

"So," she says, "what do you think?"

He's about to air his suspicions, but instead he says, "About what?"

"Being the long."

Rion shrugs. "It's about the same as being any other server, except a longer shift. At least the name's right."

She lets out a laugh. Rion glances at Doug, raises an eyebrow. He recognizes the affected falsity of Angela's laughter, even though the fluted noise is airy and authentic-sounding. She's just barely overdoing it, in such a way that anyone without any experience with such make-believe—say, anyone who hasn't been working in a restaurant long enough to see through bullshit kindness put on for the sake of a decent tip—might think she was just having a good, light-hearted time.

"I guess it isn't that different," Angela says. "Not until you close."

"I'm not sure why you'd think I'd be doing that any time soon. Unless you have plans to leave."

She shakes her head. "Of course I don't. Lifer here."

"Well, no offense, but I don't plan on being a lifer. I'm graduating next year."

"Good for you. Where will you go?"

Rion shrugs. "I don't know."

She looks at Doug. "And what about you?"

He shrugs.

"So, you could both still be here."

"Not planning on it." Rion can feel his pulse in his throat as he adds, "Unless someone does something to stop me from leaving."

Another shot of laughter, that same manufactured jocularity. Rion wants to cringe. He tries to hide the shake of his fingers as he wraps a knife and fork in a cloth napkin, rolling them up tight like he's forming a burrito. Doug, beneath the table, squeezes his thigh.

"You just never know what's coming, is all I'm saying." Angela turns toward the dining room, which is practically empty aside from two couples enjoying a final round of drinks, one with a tiramisu sitting between them, decimated, spoons turned downward astride the final remaining bite. She nods toward the bar, where Donny and Carter are still sitting. "I don't think any of them know."

"But maybe you do," Doug says.

Angela raises an eyebrow at Doug, who appears placid, the calmest Rion has ever seen him, while Rion's heart is beating as if he's just finished rushing around to a dozen tables, sweat percolating at the back of his neck.

"What do you mean?" Angela says, and even an idiot would recognize the falsity of the sick-sweetness in her voice.

Doug clears his throat. "I think—we think—you know more than anyone out there."

"Are we still talking about the future?"

Rion leans back in his seat, tries to calm himself as he crosses his arms. "I think we both know that we're not."

Something shifts in her face. It's her eyes, Rion thinks. It's always eyes. He remembers that one of his acting coaches—they didn't like to be called teachers—once said that the greatest actors are able to act with their eyes; their real self disappears and the character takes over. Look at any Academy Award winner's performance, and you'll see different eyes. Angela's have clicked, and Rion sees what might be the real her for the first time. There was always something at ease about her; she never seemed to worry or care that she was busy, had a dozen orders to expedite or checks to split or bar drinks to pick up. A halo, almost, surrounded her face, a serenity, a docility, that came from her eyes.

That is gone now. She's giving Rion a full-bore stare.

"I'm sure I don't know what you mean," she says with such primness that Rion laughs.

"Oh, I think you do." He sets down the silverware. "I've watched you."

Now a calm spreads from Angela's eyes to her lips, which have been pursed and now curl into a tiny smile. Her jaw relaxes and she leans back in her seat, arms folded across her chest, one finger of her left hand twirling her hair. "You have, have you?"

"You've never really cared about the disappearances."

"So that means I've, what, had something to do with them?" Even she seems to know not to bark out another ridiculous laugh.

Rion shrugs. "Have you?"

"You'd believe if I said yes?"

"I would."

"And if I said no?"

"Probably less likely."

She looks at Doug. "And you?"

"I'm not sure what to think. Really."

She sighs. "I've worked here a long time, you know. Ever since the restaurant opened. I'm the only one that's been here since the start."

"Okay," Rion says.

"It's an okay town, Thomasville. It's like the rest of the world. People are nice, but they aren't kind."

"I didn't know there was a difference."

"Most people don't," Angela says. "Have you ever had a table that was polite, friendly, said thank you over and over, and then left you a terrible tip?"

"All the time."

"See? Nice, but not kind. Will smile and be sweet but then when it matters won't dole out what you deserve. What you've earned."

"Can someone be kind but not nice?"

"Ah," Angela says. She turns to glance toward the dining room. "That's the right question. Take our friend Donny, for example."

Rion frowns. "Donny's okay."

She laughs, this time for real, a guttural guffaw, a sharp bark. "But no one would ever call him nice, would they?"

"I guess not."

"And yet. He cares about Carter."

Rion looks past her into the dining room. Donny and Carter are still sitting at the bar, backs curved over as they hunch toward their drinks. There's an empty stool between them. Evan is drying some wine glasses and saying something that makes both of them sit up straight and chuckle. He can't hear what's happening.

"And then there's Andre and Andrew," Angela says.

"What about them?" Rion says. "Are they nice but not kind, or vice versa?"

"Neither. Both. They're just finding themselves. And each other. Kind of like you two."

Rion swallows, his mouth feeling sour. Doug's grip on his leg tightens. They glance at one another. "So, what?" Rion says. "You did this to help us all find love?"

Angela's face is as relaxed as it's ever been. "Let me go check on my tables. I'm sure they're ready for their bills." As she stands, she leans forward as if she means to kiss him. He can smell her breath, something tropically fruity, like she's been gnashing bad chewing gum. "Don't go anywhere."

Rion rattles the silverware. "And where would I go until I'm done with this? Can't go anywhere without your sign off."

"That's correct," she says, practically gliding across the carpet to the French doors separating the back room from the dining room. When she pulls them open, Rion expects a rush of restaurant noise, but Lake | Drive is quiet.

207

Doug and Rion look at one another. Neither speaks. They aren't sure what to say. Doug lets go of Rion's hand and starts rolling a knife and fork into a napkin.

"You don't need to do that."

"What else am I going to do?"

"She doesn't seem mad at us."

"I don't think she thinks much of us." Doug twists a fork in his hand, the tines glinting in the overhead lights. "Do you think we should tell the others?"

"Do you think they'd care?"

"I don't know. What else can we do? We have to do something, right?"

Rion shrugs.

Angela comes barreling back into the room. She sits down in the same chair as before. Her posture remains prim, back straight, neck elongated like a swan.

"Just look at you two," she says, beaming.

Rion and Doug share a glance. "What about us?" Doug says.

"You're happy, aren't you?"

"About what?" Rion says.

"One another." She points a finger, painted a bright fuchsia, from Doug to Rion and then Rion to Doug. "You've found one another."

"Is that what all of this was about?" Rion says. "People finding one another?" He looks toward Doug, a little pinch in his stomach. "People falling in love?"

"Well, now that you've used the word." Angela stands and walks across the private room to its wall of windows looking out on the lake and the path that slithers toward The Drive. "I like this restaurant. I like this town. Small, quiet. Except for when the fraternities have parties, of course." She turns to them and smirks, then swivels back to the window. Her hands are clasped behind her back. "It's full of nice people."

"But not kind people," Rion says.

"But not kind. Most people in the world aren't kind. And it holds them back. And trust me, there's no fixing them as individuals."

"So you decided to fix the world," Doug says.

Angela is haloed in silver light, the moon fat and low and gibbous, hovering over the trees. "Exactly," she says, snapping a finger and pointing at Doug. "You get it. You always have, haven't you? I like that about you, Doug. I hope you go places. Places beyond these walls."

"So, you were trying to fix the world?" Rion says.

"Fix is such a loaded term." She glances into the dining room. Rion looks out, too: Carter and Donny are gone, as are Angela's last tables, the only reminders of their presence their empty martini glasses and the smeary dessert plate. Someone took the last bite. "One can't really fix the world in its entirety, even with a grand gesture."

"But you were willing to try."

She sits. "It was a thing to try out."

"But why?" Doug says. "Why make a bunch of people disappear."

"It was a change. What's the saying? 'Rome wasn't built in a day'? You can't change the world entirely in a day."

"Seems like you changed a lot," Rion says.

"But why let us remember?" Doug says.

Angela nods, as if he's asked a yes/no question. "If no one knew that things had changed, did things really change?"

"That's like the whole 'if a tree falls in a forest and no one's around to hear it, does it make a sound' thing," Rion says.

"In that case the tree has fallen," Angela says. "Someone who comes trudging by after the fact would see that the tree is on the ground. It doesn't matter if they've heard the sound or not. But would the world be any different if no one knew it was different?"

Doug's eyes go wide. "Who even knows if this hasn't happened before?"

"I do," Angela says. "It hasn't."

"How can you know that?" Rion says.

"What are you, anyway?" Doug asks.

"There's no good name for what I am."

"Are you an angel?"

She laughs, a clean peal of noise like a bell. "That would be pretty on the nose, wouldn't it?"

"So what then?" Rion says.

"Does it matter? I see the world, in all its ugliness and glory. I enrich it and it enriches me, near and far." She taps the tabletop and looks toward the windows. Cloud cover has obscured the moon. "This place is special to me."

"Thomasville?" Rion says. "The lake?"

"The restaurant?" Doug adds.

"Yes."

"Yes to which?" Rion says.

"All of them." Angela takes a deep breath. "I feel them all. I live them all. I love them all. From the grass out there to your stack of silverware. Every guest, every employee."

"Even Donny?"

She smiles. "Even Donny."

"What happens now?" Doug says.

Angela shrugs. "Why does something have to happen?"

"You can't keep things this way."

She looks at Rion. "Why not?"

He opens and closes his mouth. Doug looks at him, frowning. "What about all those people who are gone? What did you do to them?"

"Life ends and life begins."

"You killed them, then," Doug says.

"I don't know if killed is the right word. It's as if they never were."

"But we remember them," Rion says.

Doug folds his arms over his chest. "How'd you do it?"

Angela leans her elbows on the table and props her head in her hands. "If I explained that, I'm afraid your heads would explode."

Doug's shaking his head, but Rion says to him, "I think she's telling the truth." He can see it in her body language; there's no stiff affectation. The lift of her eyebrows is natural. The way her head tilts to one side, her fingers cradling her jawline.

"So now what?" Doug says.

Angela shrugs. "We see what unfolds. We're in a new world. Both here in the small and out there in the large."

"And when will you know if you've gotten the new world right?"

"I already do know. The world is definitely different."

"Is it better?" Rion says.

"That remains to be seen. Don't you think?"

Rion isn't sure what to say; he feels dried out, husked, pulled apart. Angela stands. Doug starts to speak but then stops, as if he, too, recognizes that there's nothing more to be done or said. They both watch Angela sweep across the room toward the doors, which she pulls open. She glances back at them. This feels like an ending and a beginning to Rion. Angela gives them a quick smile and a nod, and then she walks through, shutting the doors behind her. Rion and Doug sit in silence, the only sound their breathing. Doug's is wet, almost ragged, like he's panting from exertion but trying to hide it. More acting. Rion looks at him and reaches out a hand. Doug takes it and squeezes. Rion squeezes back because what else, he wonders, is there to do except that? One gesture at a time, one moment at a time, one single discovery. See what comes next.

Printed in the USA
CPSIA information can be obtained
at www.ICGtesting.com
JSHW022157110923
48293JS00011B/103